READ

BETWEEN

THE

LINES

READ

BETWEEN

THE

LINES

JO KNOWLES

CANDLEWICK PRESS

First edition 2015

Library of Congress Catalog Card Number 2014944796
ISBN 978-0-7636-6387-2

14 15 16 17 18 19 BVG 10 9 8 7 6 5 4 3 2 1

Printed in Berryville, VA, U.S.A.

This book was typeset in Nimrod.

Candlewick Press
99 Dover Street
Somerville, Massachusetts 02144

visit us at www.candlewick.com

*For the man driving the station wagon who gave my family
the finger in 2003 even though we didn't deserve it.
Thank you for inspiring this story.*

*But more importantly, for Robin Wasserman,
who encouraged me to write it.*

ONE:
FINGER BOY
(Nate: 8:15 a.m.)

I.

I STEP OUT OF THE MASS OF STINKING BODIES and get ready to catch the ball.

"Granger's open!" someone yells.

Ben Mead has it. He pivots on one foot, trying to find an opening among the hands blocking his vision. He sees me and pauses doubtfully, then looks around for someone else. Anyone else. Everyone knows passing to Granger is about as effective as throwing the ball out of bounds. Or worse, handing it over to the other team.

I raise my hands to show him Granger's ready anyway. I am wide open.

He darts his head around again. Desperate. Ben Mead is the captain of the basketball team and doesn't even need to take PE. But I guess, for him, it's an easy A.

"Give it to Granger!" another commands. It's Keith. He's always looking out for me, even though it comes at a risk. It's never a good idea to be friends with the Kcoj. That's "jock" spelled backward. Because I am the opposite of a jock.

Ben passes it to Jacob Richarde instead. He's also on the basketball team and also most likely trying to get an easy A. He dribbles a few times but gets swarmed by the other side. Without warning, he hurls the ball at me four times harder than he really needs to. Like we're back in third grade playing dodgeball and he not only wants to hit me — he wants to make it count.

I hear the break before I feel it. It's kind of a click. Like the sound my dad's fingers make when he cracks his knuckles, one by one, as he watches a fight on TV. Like he's the one getting ready to use his fists.

The basketball slips from my fingers and bounces into a mass of hands and white T-shirts, half of them covered with red mesh pinnies to show which team they're on. Ben and Jacob look at me with disgust as a red gets the ball and dribbles toward the other end of the court. The rest take chase—a sprawling, blurry candy cane. Their sneakers squeak on the gym floor. The sound echoes through the empty stands.

"Defense!" Ben yells above the squeaks. No one responds. I hate gym.

I stand alone at my end of the court, finger throbbing, and try to concentrate on not letting the water welling up in my eyes spill over.

Please, God. Not that.

I take a deep breath to calm myself, but that just seems to make the pain worse, as if proof of life makes the pain that much more unbearable.

How long does it take for a broken finger to start to swell up like a sausage? I grit my teeth against the throbbing and wait to find out.

Ms. Sawyer blows the whistle she keeps on a black cord around her neck as a second wave of pain rushes at me and brings me to my knees. The candy-cane mass beyond me becomes a pink jumble as my eyes water again. If I wasn't in so much pain, I would laugh. They are so far from *pink*.

I blink away my tears before anyone can see.

"Granger!" Ms. Sawyer yells. "What do you think you're doing?"

Her tiny body bobs toward me. Behind her, the candy-cane mob turns to finally notice they are short one guy. Not that my participation was making much difference.

Keith is the first to part from the pack and follow Ms. Sawyer up the court, ignoring one essential rule of survival: Never show the crowd you feel sorry for the Kcoj, or *you* become the Kcoj. But he's my best friend. He can't help it.

"Granger!" Ms. Sawyer yells again. It's weird how in gym class everyone resorts to using last names, like we're in the army or something. I don't see the connection. Maybe it makes us seem more tough. Most of us, anyway.

Ms. Sawyer's small head peers down at me. She tilts it to the right and squints at me the way a crow looks at a dying animal on the side of the road, soon to be roadkill.

Do I let him live, or put him out of his misery? I bet she's thinking.

Kill me now, I think back. *Please.*

She bends down and puts her hand on my shoulder. It's small and dainty. Not like you would think a gym teacher's would be.

"Let's see, kiddo," she says. *Kiddo.* Like I'm nine instead of a ninth-grader. Somehow though, coming from her, it isn't insulting. It's comforting.

She reaches for my hand, but I pull it away fast,

4

knowing it will hurt more if she touches it. Instead she bends down to get a closer look and winces. "Grab the hall pass and go to the nurse," she says. "You'll be all right."

She turns and jogs toward the candy canes. This seems to indicate that I'm not hurt that badly, and everyone goes back to ignoring me. Keith pauses and turns toward me, giving me a questioning look like, *You sure you're OK?* I give him a slight nod so no one else notices: *I'll survive.*

At this school, and especially in this gym class, one guy showing sympathy toward another guy is not recommended. At least showing sympathy toward *this* guy. And by *this guy,* I mean me.

I stand up and immediately feel woozy. The gym floor rocks to one side, then the other. I spread my legs to get my balance, as if I'm standing on the deck of a boat. Slowly, the floor steadies and I find the hall pass at the bottom step of the bleachers.

Ms. Sawyer blows her whistle again. The sneakers go back to squeaking and the shouts to *Pass it! Pass it! Pass it! Shoot!* pick up. I'm not sad to leave them.

I walk down the empty hallway slowly, savoring being able to walk without fear of being pushed or tripped.

The floor is littered with crinkled-up paper and pens with no ink.

A strip of toilet paper.

The distorted metal from a spiral notebook.

An empty Doritos bag

A crushed Gatorade bottle. Blue.

And me.

Mr. French, the head custodian, is usually so fanatical about clean hallways. Any time I leave class to hide in the bathroom or go to the nurse, I see him in the hall with his push mop, cleaning up everyone's garbage. I always try to say *hi* or *thank you,* because I imagine it is a crappy job, but whenever he sees me, he looks away and hurries down the hall. One time I bumped into him when I was rushing out of class, and he dropped his mop and kind of panicked and just stared at me like I was a ghost. Then he kept saying he was sorry, as if me bumping into him was his fault. He's a strange guy. My guess is he's out sick today because this place looks like a dump.

I reach out with my good hand and clang the locks on the locker doors, just because I can. *Clang-clang-clang.* It feels good to be bad for once. Confident.

I wish this could be me all the time, not just in the safety of an empty hall. I wish I could be more than the kid everyone likes to watch fall on his face because he's "clumsy" (they trip me). Who wears lame clothes because he's "poor" (my dad doesn't give me money to buy the right stuff). Who's a "wimp" (how does a skinny guy like me stand up to someone twice his size without being trampled?).

They don't know me.

My finger throbs with each step as I get closer to the nurse's office, which is in the same direction as the main entrance. Or exit, depending on how you look at it. I consider what would happen if I kept walking and didn't go to the nurse's office. What would happen if I slipped outside? Slipped away?

But the throbbing aches all the way up to my ear drums now, and I am so tired.

All I want to do is lie down and disappear.

II.

In the nurse's office there is a daisy-covered plastic shower curtain hanging from the ceiling to hide the vinyl-covered bed that smells like bleach and makes a farting sound when you roll over on it.

I can't wait do to that now, despite the embarrassing sound. I just want to go behind the curtain and drink from

7

the paper cone cup that makes the water taste funny and swallow the white pills that I know will barely dull the pain. I want to lean back on the farting bed and stare at the dots in the ceiling tiles and listen to the nurse make personal calls because she forgot I'm in the room, behind the curtain, pretending not to exist.

The nurse swivels around on her stool when she hears me come in. Her thick thighs bulge over it so you can't see the fake leather seat. She eyes me up and down, scanning me for what's wrong. Her eyes settle on my cradled hand, then hone in on my finger.

"Ouch," she says, wheeling herself over to me. She reaches for my hand, just like Ms. Sawyer did. She's a nurse. Doesn't she know that's a terrible idea? Why do people always want to touch what hurts?

I pull my hand out of reach.

"I need to take a look," she says, smiling in a gentle sort of way. She has eyes like a deer. They are deep brown and too big for her face. She blinks at me. She's wearing green eye shadow and thick purple mascara. The green matches her nurse's shirt.

"I won't touch it. Promise."

I step forward and hold out my swollen finger. It's even bigger than a sausage now. It makes me think of those old-fashioned cartoons of Tom and Jerry when Jerry hammers Tom on the head and a furless pink bump pops up out of his skull and pulses like a neon sign.

Womp-womp-womp.

"Hmmm," she says, squinting. Her name is Mrs. O'Connor. She darts her head around my hand, trying to see my finger from all sides. "Looks like a bad one. Think you broke it, hon?"

I remember the sound I heard when the ball hit. I'm sure there was a crack. But I don't think bones really make a sound when they break.

"I don't know," I tell her. "Could I just lie down for a while?" The floor has started to sway again.

"I wonder if you should have that X-rayed," she says, ignoring my question.

The floor sways in a new direction and I stumble a little. "No," I say. "I'm sure it's just a sprain."

She frowns.

"Couldn't I just lie down?" I ask again.

"Of course, hon. Let me call your folks and see if it's OK to give you some ibuprofen for the swelling."

I don't have folks. I have a *folk.* She should know this by now since I've spent enough time in here. Maybe it's just a word she's used to saying in the plural.

Maybe it's just wishful thinking, that there is someone else she could call besides my father. She's had to deal with that *folk* on the phone before. It couldn't possibly have been pleasant.

She glides back over to her desk. There is something graceful in how she moves across the floor on that stool, her feet pointing at the same angle, as she zooms away from me. Like she's trying to fly.

"What's the number, hon?"

I tell her.

She clicks the number using the eraser end of a pencil.

"Hello, is this Mr. Granger?" she asks. She turns to me and winks, as if to say, *I got this.*

I'm pretty sure she's about to be disappointed.

"This is the school nurse at Irving High. I have your son here with me. He hurt his hand in gym class this morning."

She's quiet while my dad replies. Then she squirms, ever so slightly.

I picture my dad on the other line, making his combination disgusted and disappointed face. It's a bit like Ben Mead's, come to think of it.

What did the hurt magnet get up to this time? I imagine him asking.

My dad thinks everyone wants to beat me up.

I wish he wasn't right.

When I was younger and still dumb enough to go to him after "getting hurt on the playground at school" (someone kicked the crap out of me), he would always have the same two reactions: "Christ, don't be such a baby" followed by "What did you do that for?" As if I had a choice. He really loved that second one. The old joke that was never funny.

"Well, no," Mrs. O'Connor says. "It's not his hand exactly." She pauses. It's like she knows what she is going to say will sound pathetic. "He hurt his finger. Actually."

Another pause. Probably while she waits for him to stop bitching about what a lost cause I am.

"It's very swollen," she says. "I think it might be broken. I'd like to give him some ibuprofen and ice it, try to get the swelling down so I can get a better look."

She squirms on her stool and turns to smile at me sympathetically, as if to say, *I'm so sorry your father is such an asshole,* even though she doesn't seem the type to use that word except in extreme cases. I shrug back like, *No worries. I can handle him.*

She looks doubtful.

"All right, Mr. Granger," she says, twisting away from me again. "I'll do that. Yes. I'll keep you posted. [Pause.] Yes, I'm sure you're busy. [Pause.] Well, it does look like a nasty injury. [Pause.] Finger injuries can be very painful, sir. [Pause.] All right. Yes. I'll call you back."

Sho hangs up the phone but waits a minute before turning around to face me again. Her shoulders and back rise up and down. Deep breaths. Calming breaths. My dad has that effect on people.

When she stands, the squished cushion seat slowly begins to inflate, erasing the indent her huge rear left on it. "He says it's fine to give you some pain relief," she says. She walks to the cupboard and unlocks it with the key she wears on a cord around her neck, similar to the one Ms. Sawyer keeps her whistle on.

She opens a bottle and empties two pills into a tiny paper cup that always reminds me of the kind you put ketchup in at the food court at the interstate rest area. I used to love stopping there on road trips with my parents. It was always my job to fill the cups with ketchup, mustard, and relish. Before my mom left, it was the best job ever. We'd share cups and dip our fries in, talking about how much fun we were going to have wherever it was we were headed. Sometimes she'd tap my nose with the end of a fry and get ketchup on me, and before I could wipe it off, she'd call me Rudolph. Then one day my dad said, "More like Bozo," and that put an end to that. Even so, my dad seemed happy then. Happy to be with my mom, at least. But that was before. The last time I went anywhere with him, I tried to carry two cups of ketchup in one hand, and they tipped and oozed down my hand and onto my new sneakers. My dad called me a "waste of space" and everyone looked at us, like they were trying to figure out if I really was, or if my father was one for calling me that. I think the jury is still out.

Mrs. O'Connor hands me the mini cup. "Let me get you some water to swallow those down with," she says. She reaches for the cone cup dispenser next to the sink and fills one up.

"Here you go, hon," she says sweetly.

Confession: I like it when she calls me *hon*. It is so much nicer than the words my dad is fond of: *Little prick. Loser. Moron. Good-for-nothing. Dumbass. Little queer. Pussy. Worthless little—*

I drop the pills onto my tongue, lift the cup to my mouth, and breathe in the familiar school water and paper smell. I swallow the pills and water in one giant gulp.

Mrs. O'Connor smiles at me again in her sympathetic way. Sometimes I think she's the only one who cares. Who understands.

I am still holding my hurt hand against my chest. It's throbbing like crazy. My finger is more swollen now and turning purple. I can almost hear the sound of the throb.

13

Womp-womp-womp.

I've seen my hand look like this before. When I was nine. It was only a year after my mom left. My dad had forced me to eat everything on my plate even though I hated everything on it. Especially the peas. They were cold and wrinkled, but he made me sit there until I ate every last one. When I finished, I very calmly brought my plate into the kitchen and washed and dried it. Then I walked to the front door.

I was leaving. For good. I had decided as I choked down the last pea. This was it. I would be homeless. I would starve. But at least I wouldn't have to eat any more cold peas while my father looked on with hatred. I couldn't understand why he tortured me. Blamed me. I knew the truth about my mom. I knew it wasn't my fault she left us. Why couldn't he?

So, I was leaving. And I wanted to go with a bang. Or, more accurately, a slam. I knew it would piss him off, but I wanted to show him I didn't care anymore. I wanted him to know I wasn't afraid. Sure, I knew he'd probably come after me. Make me pay. But maybe I could outrun him. My anger was stronger than my fear and common sense.

I gripped the edge of the door and felt the solidness of it. Then I put everything I had into slamming it closed against the House of Horror.

Somehow though, I wasn't able to move my hand away at the same time. It was as if the door itself was grabbing me. Trapping me.

I've got you. You're not going anywhere.

I felt a hot, hot pain when I finally freed myself from the door's jaw. My finger swelled up just like it is now. I bit my lips together to keep in my scream because if my father heard, if he knew I couldn't even get slamming the door right, he would laugh. He would say it served me right. And I couldn't let him say that. So I swallowed the scream and my tears and choked on the pain as I ran down the driveway and up the road. I ran and ran and wished I would never have to turn back. Never have to face the ugly mouth of That House again.

I ran until I found a stand of lilac bushes. I crawled under the lowest branches and hid there, crying privately under the green leaves, just as I did the day my mother left us. A deep hole had been dug out there by some neighborhood dog. I fit myself into the hole and wished I was that dog. A dog someone probably loved and didn't mind if he dug a hole under the lilacs to stay cool in the summer. My dad would make fun of me for knowing the name of the bushes. He would call me a sissy or mama's boy or worse.

But lilacs were my mom's favorite, so of course I

recognized them. Every spring she would cut a few sprigs and put them in a vase so the house would smell nice. "Like the promise of summer days coming," she always said. Then she would hug me close, and I could feel her hope and love settle into me.

That's how I knew what the bush was called.

I was no sissy.

Maybe I was a mama's boy, though.

Until she left me.

Then I was no one's boy.

When someone leaves unexpectedly, it has to be someone's fault. You need someone to blame. My father blamed me. He blamed me, so he hated me.

The day my mother left us, I was never his boy again. I was his burden.

When the neighbor and her dog found me in the bushes that night, I begged to be left alone. But she brought me home anyway. And that night, more than my finger throbbed with pain.

No one slams the door on my father.

But secretly, I really thought he beat the crap out of me because I came back.

Mrs. O'Connor waddles over to the refrigerator to get an ice pack for me. I glance at her very tidy desk. There's a bouquet of flowers on one corner with a card sticking out. I bet it's from her husband. On the other corner, there's a framed photo of her family. She has four kids, and she's posing with them and her husband. They're all wearing jeans and white T-shirts. They're beaming, as if they are the happiest family in the world, even if they also look like the dorkiest family in their matching outfits. The kids seem to range in age from about four to twelve or so. They all have really white teeth. I wonder if they were Photoshopped. I wonder if they are all really that happy. Probably.

"This will hurt at first," Mrs. O'Connor says as she hands me the ice pack. "But it should help with the swelling."

She pulls a piece of paper across the bed behind the curtain and puts a fresh paper case on the pillow. "Can you sit and lean against the wall? I think you should keep your hand raised above your heart for now."

I nod and adjust myself on the bed. It farts awkwardly as predicted. I lean against the cinder-block wall. It's cold and reassuringly hard. Solid. I close my eyes and feel myself disappearing, just like little kids think they do when they hide their faces. If only.

"You'll be all right," Mrs. O'Connor tells me. "Let me know if you need anything."

She pulls the curtain shut.

I listen to her nursing shoes creak under her weight as she makes her way back to the stool. The air in the cushion empties out in a quiet whistle-breath when she sits back down. She starts to hum the tune to "It's a Small World." She probably takes her family to Disney World every year. That's probably where they took that picture. That's probably why they all look so happy.

I concentrate on my pulsing finger, almost throbbing to the rhythm of the song. I sing it in my head as Mrs. O'Connor hums.

I find that song kind of depressing, to tell the truth. People like Mrs. O'Connor's kids get the laughter and hope part of the world; people like me get the rest: tears and fear.

Womp-womp-womp.

I close my eyes and pretend the invisible trick works.

After a while Mrs. O'Connor peeks her head around the curtain to check on me. "How're you doing?" she asks.

I lift the ice pack off and look. The swelling is about the same, but my finger seems to be getting more purple.

"Ooh. That's not good," she says, stepping closer to inspect.

"Does that mean I broke it?"

"Maybe. I better call your dad back. I really think you need to have it X-rayed."

I look up at the ceiling and sigh. She pats my knee. "It'll be OK," she says.

But I don't know what she means by *it.*

She goes to make the call. It takes about two seconds to figure out that my dad is not happy.

"Well, it does look pretty bad," Mrs. O'Connor says quietly. Pause. "Yes, I really think he needs to have an X-ray. [Pause.] No, I can't tell just by looking. But I've seen a lot of broken fingers over the years, sir." Her voice gets louder. "No, I'm not a doctor. [Pause.] All right. Yes. He'll be here. We'll see you soon."

I brace myself for the look on her face when she pulls the curtain back again.

"He's such a dick," I tell her, surprising myself with my choice of words. "Sorry."

"I don't like that talk," she says. But she pats my knee again and smiles. Code for *But, yes. He really is.*

I lean my head back against the hard wall and close my eyes again.

Here is my fantasy:

I'm sitting with my dad in the waiting room at the hospital. It's full of people moaning about whatever pain it is that brought them there. My father will appear physically uncomfortable having to be near so many people, especially people who are "bellyaching." I will enjoy watching him squirm. A hot nurse walks into the room. She's holding a clipboard. She scans the list on it and calls out, "Nathan Granger?" My father and I will both stand up at the same time because my name is the one and only thing we share. But the nurse will check me out, not my dad. She'll smile and give me a sexy look and say, "Come with me," in this really suggestive way, and I will smile back at her and then give my father a very fake-sorry face. The hot nurse and I will disappear down the hall together, leaving my father alone with all the drug addicts and runny-nose coughing little kids. Instead of taking me to some tiny little cubicle with curtains for walls, the nurse will take me to a supply closet. She'll tell me how hot I am and start to undress and say how she wants to be the one I lose my virginity to and how she's going to make sure I never forget my first time and . . .

Mrs. O'Connor starts humming "It's a Small World" again.

I shift uncomfortably on the squeaky bed and try to think other thoughts before she sees what else is suddenly swollen.

Oh, God.

I concentrate on the pain in my finger instead. The paper crinkles under me. Then I hear a click on the other side of the curtain. It's the sound of the office door opening.

"Well, hello, Claire. How are you doing, honey?"

The curtain is closed so I can't see who's on the other side, but I only know one Claire. Claire Harris. And she is even better than my fantastical hot nurse.

"Hi, Mrs. O'Connor," she says.

"How can I help you, hon?"

I'm kind of surprised to hear her call someone else *hon*. I thought that was just for me.

"Uh," Claire says quietly. "I have cramps."

I wish I hadn't heard that.

"Aw, hon," Mrs. O'Connor says again. It's kind of bugging me.

"They're really bad. Can I call my mom?"

"Sure, sweetie. I'd let you lie down, but the bed's occupied."

Claire peers through the curtain.

Oh. My. God.

"Hey," she says. She doesn't seem to be embarrassed by the fact that I know she's having her period.

"Hey," I say, but it comes out like a high-pitched croak.

21

"What happened to your hand?"

Claire Harris just asked me a question. Claire Harris is *talking* to me. Keith is going to die of jealousy.

"Gym," I say. I lift off the ice and we both gasp. My finger is hideous.

"Wow. That looks, like, really bad," she tells me.

"He's going to the hospital as soon as his dad gets here," Mrs. O'Connor says. "Do you want to sit down while I call your mom, Claire? What's the number?"

Claire sits next to me on the bed and recites her number. The bed doesn't fart when Claire Harris sits on it. It's like even the bed has standards. I'm a little offended, but I also understand. It's *Claire Harris* after all. Sitting ten inches away from me. So close I can smell her perfume. It smells like . . . grass? Summer. It's nice. Like outside.

"Hi, Mrs. Harris, this is Mrs. O'Connor from school. I've got Claire here, and she's not feeling well. [Pause.] That's right. [Pause.] Oh, I know. We ladies just can't get a break."

Claire sighs and stares up at the ceiling. She seems unaffected by the topic of conversation, but my face is burning hot.

"She wants to go home, if that's all right with you? [Pause.] The bus? [Pause.] OK. I'll tell her."

Claire stands up as soon as Mrs. O'Connor gets off the phone. I try not to look anywhere near her . . . reproductivo area.

Oh. My. God.

"I'm gonna go now," Claire says. She picks up the bag she left on the floor and swings it over her shoulder. Her hair gets caught in the strap and she pulls it out. It cascades down her back like she's in a shampoo commercial.

"Be safe, hon," Mrs. O'Connor says.

"I will." She turns to me and smiles. "Hope your finger's OK, um. Sorry. What's your name?"

"Nate," I say.

"Nate." She smiles again. Then she leaves.

"Pretty girl," Mrs. O'Connor says, raising her eyebrows. "A little old for you, though, I suppose."

"And a little too hot," I say.

She laughs.

"Looks aren't everything, hon." Even if it's a little less special now, I still like it when she calls me that.

The door opens again, and this time there is a bitterness that blows in with it. It does not smell like grass and the outdoors. It smells like my father. Like aftershave and stale cigarettes.

"Hi, Mr. Granger," Mrs. O'Connor says. She pulls the

curtain all the way open with a loud swish as the rings slide harshly across the bar. My father sees me and my finger and shakes his head.

"Doesn't look *that* bad," he says.

It never does, Dad.

I glance over at the nurse, who looks like she just smelled something gross.

My dad leans closer. "Let me see it." He starts to reach for my hand.

I hold it out to his ugly frown to keep him from getting too close to me.

"It's not even that swollen," he says, turning to Mrs. O'Connor. "You really think he broke it?"

She sighs. "I don't know for *sure*. But yes. That would be my guess. Fingers aren't supposed to be purple."

Good one, Mrs. O.

He squints at my finger. Any idiot can see it is a strange shade of purple and three times bigger than the others. Slowly, I curl down my pinkie and ring finger. Then my pointer and thumb, so that I'm holding my fingers inside a fist aimed at my dad. All but one finger, that is.

And my God, even though it hurts like hell to do it, because moving any of my fingers causes shooting pain up my arm, it is worth it. It is worth it to stick my big, broken purple middle finger up at my father. To stick it right in his face.

I grin.

He frowns.

We stare.

Finally, it dawns on him what I *might* be doing. He looks confused. Would I really have the balls to give him the finger? Would I dare? We both know he wouldn't hesitate for one second to smack me across the face right here if he thought I was. Screw the nurse. Screw what she would think.

I stop smiling at the image and think the words my finger is saying. The words I have longed to say to him every time he boxes my ears. Every time he laughs when I make a mistake. Every time he calls me the name I refuse to repeat. Every time I call to invite a friend over and they say no and give some lame excuse, never acknowledging that it isn't because they don't like me but because they're terrified of my father. How are you supposed to make friends in a situation like that?

Maybe I am a Worthless Little___. But I'm only a Worthless Little___ because of you, Dad.

He grunts, deciding I don't have the balls after all. "Let's go, then," he says. "I don't have all day. This is already costing me at work."

See?

I stand up and feel dizzy but quickly find my balance before my dad can see me stumble. Be weak. Mrs. O'Connor gives me a sympathetic look.

"No worries," I say. I even wink at her. I have never winked at anyone before. But this strange feeling of ballsiness has come over me.

I hold my hand and finger up behind my dad and smirk.

I don't know why, but somehow I feel like something good is going to come out of this injury after all.

III.

In the cab of my dad's truck, we stare straight ahead, not speaking. I hold my hand upright across my chest and crack the window open to keep from getting sick from the smell of his cigarettes. He quit before I was born, when he met my mom, but picked right back up the day she left. He huffs and puffs with his window rolled up, just to torture me, I swear.

I open my window and, like a dog, lift my face to the breeze just to torture him back.

Every so often my dad sighs uncomfortably. He never asks if I'm OK. This isn't a surprise. Just an observation.

We pull into the parking lot and park near the emergency entrance.

"Let me see that again," he says.

I lift my middle finger toward him and think the words when he makes his disgusted face.

"It dooon't look that bad," he says again.

"Then let's just go home," I dare him.

He looks up and squints at the hospital entrance. He takes an awkward breath and chokes. I wait for him to pull out another cigarette, but he keeps his hands on the wheel.

I wait.

He waits.

We both eye the pack between the seats, and he instinctively grabs it and opens his door.

"Let's get this over with," he says. He lights up and starts puffing as he walks toward the entrance.

I follow silently.

We pause when we step on the sensor that opens the door. He turns to me and looks at my finger one more time. He takes another long drag. Then another. The embers glow bright, and I think he'll swallow the thing whole if he's not careful.

"You sure it could be broken?" he asks seriously.

The question takes me by surprise. So does the look on his face. It's more than annoyance. Or anger. He looks scared.

We both gaze at the door, and I realize why he's so nervous. Because I remember this, just like he's probably remembering. The two of us, standing here on another horrible day, somehow both knowing the terrible news waiting on the other side. And now it suddenly feels terrifying to move forward.

I look down at my mangled finger.

"I don't know," I say. "I'm sorry."

"Forget it," he says, dropping the still-glowing cigarette to the ground next to the butt bin. He doesn't bother to stomp it out. He steps forward bravely and walks inside.

He's gruff with the nurse at the admissions desk. She's gruff back.

We find seats in the waiting room once the nurse puts a plastic bracelet with my name on it around my wrist. I sit first, at a seat where I can watch the TV that hangs from the ceiling in one corner. My father chooses a seat next to some other empty chairs across the room instead of the one next to me. Could be he just doesn't want to watch Fox News. Could be he just doesn't want to sit next to his embarrassment of a son. Whatever.

There's a lady sitting in the corner with her daughter. The girl rests her head on her mom's shoulder. They're holding hands. I try to remember what that felt like. My mom's hand in mine. Reassuring. Calm. Safe. When she took my hand, I felt loved.

I press my throbbing hand to my chest and glare at my father, who sits restlessly on the other side of the room.

I try to see him as a stranger would. His hair is trimmed close to his scalp. Not quite a crew cut but almost. He is clean shaven. He has no laugh lines. The wrinkles between his eyebrows are from making his angry face. His mouth is set in a scowl. He appears to be reading *Time* magazine, but probably he's just looking at the pictures. He's flipping through the pages way too fast for anything else. Hyper. I can tell he needs a cigarette by the way his hands tremble when he turns the pages.

Chillax, I imagine saying. *You're not the one with the smashed finger.*

He glances up and looks around the room. His knee

bounces nervously. He gives me the evil eye. *It's all your fault I'm here.* I can hear him thinking. *It's always your goddamned fault.*

It dawns on me that he's probably right. The last time he was here, in this very room, he was waiting for news about my mom. Waiting and hating me. Blaming me. Wishing it was me in the ER, not her.

It's my fault she got in the car that day. She didn't like me taking the bus. She didn't like the bruises I acquired on my ride home. Besides, she said, she liked picking me up at school. She liked to be able to check in with the teachers and other parents. It was a social thing, she insisted, whenever my dad questioned her. But she and I both knew, and maybe my dad did too, that she was really trying to protect me from the daily torture I was sure to get on the bus.

Even though I know it's not rational, I ask the *maybe* questions too. Maybe it *was* my fault. Maybe I should have told her I liked taking the bus. Maybe if just that one day I'd told her I wanted to.

But I didn't.

And she died.

She died a horrible, painful death right here. In this hospital. Because some person drank too much and got in a car and crashed into her.

30

My dad can't blame the *driver,* though.

Because we never found out who it was.

The police said that judging from the marks in the road, the person was probably wasted. "Typical hit-and-run," they said.

I hate that phrase.

It sounds like a baseball game.

Not murder.

It's too hard to blame a nameless, faceless person, even though I suppose we've both tried. In the end, it's easier to blame me. I know.

"Nathan Granger?" a guy nurse walks into the room. So much for my earlier hot nurse fantasy. Guess I won't be losing my virginity today after all. Surprise.

I stand up.

"Ouch," the nurse says. "That's gotta hurt."

"Yeah," I say. I glance over at my dad. He doesn't look up from his pretend reading.

"Are you with a parent?" the nurse asks.

"My dad," I say.

Finally my dad looks up from the magazine.

"Would you like to come with us, Mr. Granger? Or wait here?"

"I'll wait outside in the truck," he tells me. "You

can call me if you need me to sign anything and I'll
come in."

The nurse looks at him like he is a first class asshole.

"Will it be long?" my dad asks. "I really need to get
back to work."

"I don't know," the nurse says in a syrupy-sweet
voice.

My father grimaces at the sound. I know what he's
thinking: *Queer.*

He's called me that enough times.

"We'll try to be as quick as we can," the nurse adds.
He turns to me. "Let's go take a look and see what we're
dealing with."

Before I follow him out, I watch my dad rush toward
the exit. There's something about the way he hurries out
that is different from the way he normally moves. If I
didn't know better, I'd swear he was terrified.

Maybe it really wasn't the need for a nic fix causing
his hands to shake.

Maybe he just can't bear to be in this place again.

I walk behind the nurse through a maze of halls until we
get to a tiny curtained space with a bed next to a bunch
of machinery.

"I'm just going to take your blood pressure and all that boring stuff. Then we'll get you X-rayed."

I nod. He punches some keys on a tiny laptop.

"So, how'd this happen?" he asks.

"In gym. I'm crap at basketball."

He laughs. "Yeah, me too."

When he finishes with the basics, he makes me get in a wheelchair and pushes me down a whole new set of mazes until we get to the X-ray area.

"You might have to wait awhile, but I'll be back when you're done. Want a magazine or something?"

"No worries," I say.

He leaves me alone in the hall. There's an empty stretcher and a line of wheelchairs against one wall. I imagine all the different patients who've sat in those chairs. The kids with the broken legs, arms, and fingers. I imagine most of them would have a parent by their side, not left all alone like me. I picture my father back in his truck, cursing me. Checking his watch every two minutes, getting all amped up about how much work he's missing. Chain-smoking like a fiend. I'm sure it'll be a pleasant drive home.

Finally, the lab-tech person comes out and looks at the chart attached to my wheelchair.

"Nathan?" she asks, then checks my wristband. She is almost as hot as the nurse from my fantasy.

"That's me," I say.

"C'mon. We'll see if that's broken. Wanna make any bets?"

"How about wishes?"

"Depends on your wish," she says. "You don't really *want* it to be broken, do you?" She has a dimple in her right cheek. Not on her left. I think I'm in love with it.

"Well," she continues, "even if it is, there's not much they can do for you. Give you a splint and strict orders not to bang it again, at least till it heals."

I nod and follow her into the room. She puts a heavy apron around me. "No chance you're pregnant, right?" she jokes.

"No chance in hell," I say.

"TMI, my young friend," she says, tightening the apron around me.

We laugh. I wonder how old she is. She looks in her early twenties. She smells good. Like lilacs, actually. This seems very implausible, I know. Maybe my brain is just telling me that's what she smells like. Either way, I take it as a good sign.

I think about my mom again. Not because of the hot lab tech (that would be gross), but because of the smell of lilacs. Obviously. I think about the very few memories I have of her. How she used to make me hold her hand whenever we went for a walk. And how she ruffled my hair and said I belonged to the Clean Plate Club any time I ate everything on my plate. The memories are still so vivid. But I wonder how long they'll stay that way. I was only eight when she left.

When she died.

The lab tech adjusts my arm under the camera and says, "Don't move." I nod and realize that counts. "Not so fast, are you?" she says, smiling. She wags her finger at me in a joking sort of way. In a mom-ish sort of way. I breathe in her perfume one more time before she leaves me and goes inside the booth to click the scan machine. I hope she doesn't notice and think I'm a perv.

From the booth, she speaks through a mic and reminds me to be still while she takes the X-rays. Then she comes out and adjusts my arm again.

When we're finally done, she brings me the wheelchair, and the nurse comes back and wheels me to the curtained room again to wait for a doctor. After what seems like hours, a doctor finally comes in, followed by my father and a strong draft of cigarette smell. I automatically sit up straighter on the uncomfortable folding bed the nurse left me on.

"It's definitely broken," the doctor says. "But the good news is, the break's nice and clean. I'll have Christian fix you up, and you'll be good to go. You'll have to wear a splint for a few weeks and then come back for another X-ray to make sure everything's healing properly. But no more basketball for you for a while, I'm afraid."

"No problem," I say. "I suck anyway."

My dad grunts, and I regret saying it. Christian laughs. "There's more to life than being a good ball player," he says.

Tell that to my dad, I think.

But then I realize he just did.

IV.

We don't talk on the drive home. I stare out the window and hold my newly wrapped hand against my chest. Every so often, my father sighs his sigh, and I'm sure he's having thoughts of disappointment. I'm sure he always dreamed he'd have the kind of son who was the school football star. The guy who gave swirlies to guys like me.

The guy with the hot girl under his arm. The guy with muscles and nice teeth. The guy everyone loved and wanted to be.

Instead he got me.

I've never liked sports, even before he made me believe I sucked at them. I've always been afraid of balls, especially when someone is throwing one at my face. It was obvious by the time I lost a few baby teeth that I needed some serious orthodontic attention, but my father wasn't about to pay for that. And now, at four-teen, I weigh one hundred sixteen pounds. My portrait is basically the anti-boy of the one my father imagined being enshrined on our wall, which, instead, is bare and trophy-less.

There are so many reasons to resent me. Sometimes I wonder if he would have preferred that the accident happened on the way home, when I was in the car, too. Sometimes I wonder if he secretly wishes it had been me who died.

As we drive, it dawns on me that we are not actually driving in the direction that will bring us home. He's tak-ing me back to school. With a broken finger. Typical. I don't say anything because I know the response. "Suck it up. Be a man."

My stomach growls. I haven't eaten anything yet today. I never eat breakfast on gym days for fear of puking from overexertion. We "wasted" several hours at the hospital, and now I missed lunch period. What's the point of going back when school's practically over? Even so, in five minutes, we're driving into the school parking lot and up to the drop-off lane in front of the school.

My father doesn't ask how I'm feeling. He doesn't even say, *Have a nice day.* Or, *See you at home. I'll get your favorite takeout!* I don't think he would even know what that is.

Instead, he waits quietly for me to get out, his cigarette dangling a long gray tip of ash that is about to fall onto the floor of the truck. I watch it, waiting. But he doesn't notice. He just stares out the window.

"What is it, Dad?" I ask.

He keeps staring.

"Dad," I say again.

He slowly turns his head to me, as if waking from a sad dream. The ash starts to bend. It's hanging on by some miracle now.

"Your cigarette," I say, nodding my head toward it.

He presses it into the ashtray.

I wait, but he doesn't say anything.

"I'm sorry," I say.

He glances at my hand. My finger. Pointing at him. Flipping him off in the most pathetic way possible.

He nods.

I study his face in this rare moment where we acknowledge each other's presence. The crease between his eyes is deep and seems to get deeper before my eyes.

I wonder, with a horrible pang of regret, if it isn't an anger line after all. What if it's a sad line, made by grief?

"Go on," he says to me, not as harsh as usual. Or, maybe, for the first time, I'm just reinterpreting the tone.

Maybe I've been misinterpreting it all along.

I lower my finger so it's not pointing at him.

I want to say something. Ask him something. But what?

"Get going," he finally tells me. His old gruff self is back.

I get out of the truck and listen to the sound of the tires on the pavement as he drives away from me. I don't turn around. I don't think, as I so often do when he leaves me anywhere: *I hate you.*

I just think: *Good-bye.*

V.

I walk slowly to the school entrance and pause. Contemplate turning around and walking someplace else. Maybe the park. Maybe the mall. Maybe anywhere. Else.

But of course I go in. My dad's no dummy. I am a wimp. But for some reason, I don't care what he thinks anymore. For some reason, I get now that all my life, he's needed me to be the weak one. The one he can blame. I can accept that, from him. But not from anyone else. Not anymore.

In the office, the school secretary takes one look at me and my hand and cringes. "What happened, dear?"

I didn't know people still used the word *dear*. It makes me want to cry. Sometimes, when someone is nice to you for no reason but when you need it most, that happens. It's rare for me, but today seems to be one of those days. I blink my eyes. *You really are a wimp,* I think. But then I stop myself. Who cares? So I'm a wimp. There are worse things.

"Broken," I tell her.

"Shouldn't you be home resting?"

I shrug.

"Well, let me write you a pass, and you can go on to class. Unless you want to spend the rest of the day in the nurse's office? That's what I would do," she adds quietly.

"It's OK," I say. Her smile gives me an uncomfortable lump in my throat. I'm not used to this much niceness in one day.

She hands me the pass.

"Thanks," I mutter through the lump.

I purposefully tilt my finger so its pointing sideways and clearly not giving any unintended messages to her. I contemplate stopping by the nurse's office to let her know she was right about the break, but I'm not sure I can handle anyone else being nice. I swallow down the lump, get ahold of myself, and head to class.

Sixth period means Creative Writing with Ms. Lindsay. She is by far the hottest teacher in the school. But she is also, for reasons I don't understand, one of the biggest targets for torture. Usually that level of treatment is reserved for the subs, but Ms. Lindsay gets the sub treatment every day. Maybe it's because she's sort of a sub, having replaced a teacher who died last year. Not only that, but he committed suicide. People always feel guilty about suicides, even though they have nothing to do with them. I guess they think being mean to Ms. Lindsay is a sign of loyalty? I don't know. I don't understand most of the assholes in this school.

I open the door to the room and flash my pass at Ms. Lindsay, then raise my injured hand to explain my absence. I'm careful, again, not to point my finger upward. She nods and I take my usual seat in the back. All heads swivel to check me out. There's snickering, until I aim my injury toward the sound.

Keith gives me a *You OK?* look, and I nod just enough to give him my *Yeah* look.

Yeah, I'm OK.

Then there's real laughter.

I brace myself for insults, but they don't come.

The funny thing is, for the first time, the laughter is *for* me, not at me. It has the tone of admiration more than anything else.

Cal Hogan in the next seat leans toward me.

"How's it feel to be able to give the finger to anyone you want and get away with it?" he whispers.

I grin as the question sinks in.

"What do you think?" I ask.

I'm surprised by how coy and confident I sound. I sit up straighter.

I imagine myself as someone other than the school punching bag. The wimp no one cares about. The Kcoj.

Instead, I picture myself as the football jock of my father's dreams. The one everyone admires. This must be what it would feel like to be that guy. With everyone wishing they could be you for a day.

Ms. Lindsay catches my eye. She's standing nervously in front of the room, trying to get everyone's attention. She appears to be on the verge of saying something important. She seems a little scared. She looks like how I feel most days. Until now. Maybe it's time for both of us to change our ways.

Her eyes dart around the room, as if she's trying desperately to connect to someone, anyone, who will listen.

I decide to be that person.

Like her, I look around the room. I pause at each student and search the file in my brain for the mean comment, push, or kick each one has given me over the years. The ones who laughed at me, looked at me like I was a speck, called me a loser. Made me feel like one. I look at them now, as they look back at me in this new way. Like they are measuring this me against the one they vaguely remember. I was always so forgettable—just something to give a shove as they passed by.

I smile confidently and I flip them all off.

For me, and for Ms. Lindsay too.

Up in front of the room, her eyes finally settle on

mine. I watch as they move to my hand and settle on my finger.

"Finger Boy!" someone whispers loudly.

I watch the realization come over Ms. Lindsay's face.

I smile at her.

She smiles at me.

And then I burst out laughing.

TWO:
SIGN
LANGUAGE
(Claire: 9:22 a.m.)

I.

LIAR.

That's what I see in the reflection of the huge glass doors at the front of the school. We stand there, not moving. Me and my reflection. Hating each other.

I clutch the likely germ-infested handle but can't seem to push it. Reflection me is trapping real me. Pushing in while I push out. We are at a standstill. Not coming or going. I would probably still be trapped here if not for the man who appears on the other side of the door and pulls it open, ripping mirror me out of my grasp. I step aside. He doesn't acknowledge me. He looks angry and impatient. A trail of cigarette smoke swirls around me in his wake, forcing me out into the fresh air. The door slowly swings closed behind me.

Now what?

Home. I'm supposed to go home because I have cramps.

Only I don't. That was a lie.

I'm fine. At least, in that department.

So . . . what now? What should this liar do?

I've never been good at being bad.

I usually blush when I lie. I fidget. I fumble. And then I usually come clean.

But that's because the only people I've ever really lied to are my parents. Tiny lies. Like about whether or not I have homework. Or who will be in the car when I ask if I can go to a movie with Grace and the girls. But I always end up feeling guilty and confessing, and then my parents tell me they appreciate my honesty and forgive me.

But today I lied to one of the nicest ladies I know.

I blame the girls.

This morning, at our usual meet-up spot before classes, they were all there before me: Grace, Sammy, and Lacy. They were in the huddle. Usually when they see me, they open up and let me in. They give me a hug and tell me they love whatever I'm wearing, even if they don't. That's a white lie, so it doesn't count.

46

Only when I got close, they didn't open up. They said, "Hey, Claire," and instead of making space for me, broke up the circle and walked away.

I went to class alone. I don't have first period with any of them anyway, so it's not that unusual, but it still *felt* unusual. All through class, I sat there, fake-listening to Ms. Yung talk about Web design and the importance of HTML something-something-something, wondering—and then remembering—why my friends all hate me now.

"Claire," Ms. Yung had said, walking over to me, "are you listening?"

I looked up at her and noticed that she had a poppy seed between her front teeth.

"Sorry," I said, trying not to stare.

She turned and went back to talking about the magic of coding, and I sank deeper in my chair, trying to figure out how I could just go home. I couldn't face the girls again. They had every right to hate me.

So I went to the nurse's office and made my escape.

But now what?

I walk to the bus stop and study the map and various routes the buses go. The red line leads to my neighborhood. The yellow breaks off to another part of town. The green goes to the city center. I reach out and trace it with my finger.

Behind me, a bus rolls up. Without thinking or even looking for which number it is, I get on. I will go where it takes me. I told the girls I wanted more to life. Now I guess I'm going to find out what that means.

The driver smiles at me when I slide my pass card through the reader. He has a giant silver front tooth. I like it. I don't know why. Maybe because I can hear Grace or one of the other girls thinking, *Gross*. And today I am feeling the opposite of one of the girls.

We pull onto the street, and I wait to see where we end up. The usual packed bus of high-schoolers is mostly empty. I glance around and take stock of who's here. A mom or nanny with a little kid. A few businesspeople. A few more old people. I play the game I always play, making up who each one is. Who's happy. Who's sad. Who's bored. I imagine their stories based on how they're dressed and what they do to occupy themselves. The guy obsessively checking his phone for messages clearly wants a girlfriend to text him. The old lady with the paper who keeps huffing and puffing angrily is obviously a liberal who used to go on protests in the sixties and now is diminished to public grunting. She takes a pen from her enormous purse and madly scribbles out a face in a photo. I strain to see whose. The headline says something about the Republican senator from Arizona. I smirk and the lady winks at me.

"Makes me feel better," she says. "I'm not really violent."

I nod agreeably, suddenly feeling a partnership with her.

Let's change the world, I want to say to her. *I know you don't know me, but let's hijack this bus and go protest something. I don't even care what. I just feel like yelling. I just feel like caring about something.*

Anything.

But the lady has gone back to her scribbling. And now she's humming a sweet tune while she does so. And I realize the scratching out of faces is as far as her commitment goes.

I lean my head against the dirty glass and stare out the window.

It was like this last weekend, too. Me, with my head against the window, wanting to get out. Wanting anything but the right then of the endless night.

I was in Grace's car with the girls. I hate that name for us. But that's what everyone calls us. That's what we say. Or did say, anyway. "The Girls." Like we all make up one living mass instead of being individual people. First, it was Grace, Sammy, me, and Leslie. But Leslie moved away and was recently replaced by Lacy. I don't know the rules for who gets to be one of us. I don't even know how we became an us. We just always have been. Ever since we were little.

We were driving around in Grace's car, looking for the party Grace's boyfriend, Ben, was supposedly at, which he said was for "guys only." He goes to a lot of this kind of party.

We were driving for what felt like hours. The conversation never veered from each of us sharing our thoughts on where this party might be, who might be there, and what they might be drinking and saying and eating and playing and listening to.

Question: How much time can a group of supposedly smart and interesting girls spend talking about all the possible places a girl's boyfriend might be (hiding)?

Answer: An unbearably long time.

The better question and discussion should have been: Why is Grace dating such a jerk?

I didn't talk much. I never do. But the more they talked and the less I did, I began to fantasize about unbuckling my seat belt, opening the door, and falling into the street.

Instead, I stared out the window. At streetlights. Through windows of houses with lights on but shades not drawn. A hopeful glimpse of a life less mundane. But all I saw was a man eating dinner alone at a table. A family sitting in the TV light, staring at a flat box containing something more interesting than their entire darkened house. Than their entire neighborhood, entire city. Surrounded by the world, but focused on a box.

It was getting more depressing by the minute. But it was still less depressing than the back of Grace's head and the nonstop chatter of the other girls in the car, which I'd been trying to tune out for miles.

Why don't people come with mute buttons?

And when did I become such a horrible friend?

"Don't you guys ever want to talk about something meaningful?" I finally blurted out after what seemed like the seven hundredth time Grace had said, "Oh my God, why isn't he replying to my texts?"

The car grew silent.

"What do you even mean, Claire?" Lacy asked, all clueless.

"I'm sorry my love life isn't meaningful enough for you, Claire," Grace whined.

Inside, my stomach was curling in on itself. I felt like I was going to throw up.

It's not love, I wanted to tell her. But instead I said, "Just forget it."

I rested my head against the cold glass window. Beside

me, Sammy just sighed. She'd been a bit more quiet than usual, too. I suspected she might also be looking for more meaningful discussion but was afraid, or didn't care enough, to say so.

"I'll talk about something meaningful," Lacy said, mostly under her breath.

"What did you say, Lacy?" Grace asked.

But it wasn't really a question.

"Nuh-nothing," Lacy said.

I didn't know what she was so afraid of. Not until this morning, when the girls didn't welcome me into the circle.

Now I know.

Before today, I had this life. This predictable life. This bored life. This life in which I was a small part of something only slightly greater called "the Girls." This life I wanted more from.

Now my life has shifted. But instead of feeling glad or excited, I feel lost. I didn't realize how *alone* alone would feel.

I wonder, are any of the people on this bus guessing my story the same way I guessed theirs?

Here is what I think they see:

An average girl living an average life. Every day

she experiences the same meaningless thing. She goes to school. She attends classes. She eats lunch at the same table with the same friends. They eat the same thing every day. Lettuce with fat-free ranch dressing. Don't feel sorry for them. They've gotten used to it. They attend more classes. They pass each other in the halls and roll their eyes like this is the most agonizingly boring, torturous, unfair life. After school, they go to cheerleading practice. In the locker room, they talk about who looked at them the wrong way or in an interested way or any way at all. They practice their cheer routines. They go home. They do their homework. They eat dinner. They call each other until their parents tell them to stop. Then they text each other from under the covers and stay up too late, gossiping about things they should never put in writing. But they trust each other not to share. They finally drift off to sleep. They get up the next day and do it again.

If that is the picture these passengers see when they look at me, then they are right. Can anyone really blame me for wanting more?

Here is what they don't see:

Nothing.

II.

I lift my head from the glass when the bus stops. I realize
now that we are headed into the city. More people climb
aboard and we move on, picking up larger clusters of passengers as we go, until the bus is packed and we are in
the heart of downtown. I look out the window and wait
for something interesting to call me off this ride.

It's a bookstore café that finally lures me. I don't normally go to cafés. At least not alone. The girls sometimes
drag me in and try to act cool like they know how to order
a venti latte half-caf something or other, but it is all foreign to me. I bet it is to them, too.

I don't even like coffee.

I don't drink tea, either. It makes me need to pee
every ten minutes.

But today, especially, I like the idea of going inside
and sitting at a table all by myself. Without Grace,
Sammy, and Lacy.

Just me.

I like the idea of reading a book or writing in my journal, as if I have something important to say. If the girls
don't want to talk about something interesting, maybe I
could write something interesting instead. Maybe I could

come to the same café every day. Maybe I could become a regular and make friends with the other regulars. We could have friendly arguments about politics. Or discuss obscure, independent movies that we pretend to understand. And books. We could talk about and share them with each other. It could all be so romantic. So artsy. So beyond high school. So much more than driving around in Grace's car looking for Grace's boyfriend and wondering why Grace's boyfriend hasn't texted Grace.

Because I just can't do that anymore.

I open the door to the café.

It's not really the café of my imagination. There isn't a worn wooden floor, and there are no candles sticking out of old wine bottles on the tables. The chairs match. There is no comfy couch where a hipster couple plays Scrabble while sipping cappuccinos. No bookcase with a handwritten note saying: "Free to borrow and absorb." Instead, the café is a bit more like a cafeteria. I consider walking out. But it's warm, and the music is nice. Different. Dreamy. I stay.

There's a menu board above the counter, and I try to decipher the choices. I'm always forgetting the difference between a cappuccino, latte, espresso, macchiato . . . they all sound so pretentiously similar.

The man behind the counter smiles at me. What do they call coffee guys? A barista. No, that sounds female. Barister? No, that sounds stupid. Either way, he's shockingly cute.

"What can I get for you?" he asks. He has a nose ring. I like it.

"A latte, please?"

I don't even know what that is.

"Regular milk or skim?"

Is he offering skim because he thinks I'm fat?

I can't believe I just thought that. I sound like Grace or Sammy in my head.

Stop. I always drink skim. Just order skim!

"Um, skim?"

"You got it."

He takes forever to make the drink. He shakes his hips to the jazz music as he moves a green mug from machine to machine. He's wearing faded black jeans and a fitted black T-shirt. His arm muscles are just right. Not too big, not too small. He has a silver thumb ring. And a tattoo on his arm of a sunburst.

When he finally hands me my mug, there's a light-brown heart made out of cinnamon on top of the foam. He winks at me.

"Enjoy," he says, smiling. Even his teeth are nice.

I thank him and carry my drink to a table, my heart beating in a way it never has before. I pick a table in the corner and sit with my back to the wall so I can observe the people around me. I slip my journal out of my bag. It's black, with line-less pages. And it is empty.

I touch the thick ivory paper waiting for me to tell it a story with my pen. Or my political thoughts. Or my desires. Or a secret.

It waits and waits.

I take a careful sip of my coffee but burn my tongue anyway. It tastes terrible. Bitter and unsweetened. I look up and catch Barista Boy watching me. He gives me a thumbs-up with a look like, *Do you like the delicious drink I made especially for you?* So I return the thumbs-up and flash him my newly acquired liar's smile.

Then I realize I have a foam mustache.

Barista Boy grins and goes back to barista-ing.

I glance around at the people sitting nearby. They hide behind their laptops or else talk loudly with a table-mate because obviously what they are talking about is so important that the rest of the room should "overhear" and be impressed. I listen for something interesting, but all I hear are complaints about bosses, a long list of ingredients for the most amazing vegetarian strata some guy made last night (what's strata?), and a bad review of a movie I didn't catch the name of.

On my table, the open pages of my journal stare back at me, bored. Waiting. It's not a real journal. It's a mini sketchbook with wide spiral rings. If you look very closely, you can see the fibers in the paper. When I write on it with my Sharpie, the bright-blue ink bleeds just a little and makes my careful letters look like art, even though I never could draw.

The problem is, however, that all I have written is the day's date. That's all I've got. What could I possibly have to say besides, *I'm bored. Please talk to me about anything but Grace's boyfriend.*

Sometimes I feel like such a jerk.

I think about what most girls my age would write in a journal. What Grace might write. Or Sammy. Or Lacy. It's awful of me, but I imagine the worst. Grace would write her name with Ben's last name. With hearts around it. And then, maybe on the next page in impossibly small letters, she would write the truth. That she knows Ben doesn't love her. That he tries to hide from her. That he lies about the parties and laughs with his friends when they find out she and her own friends drive around every weekend looking for a party that doesn't exist. That sometimes he is secretly hiding out with Lacy's ex–best friend, Stephen. That once Grace saw them kissing. She told me. In a moment of weakness and desperation, followed by a moment of clarity and regret and "I mean it *looked* like they were, but they probably totally *weren't.* Oh my God, I can't believe I even thought that. Never mind. Please don't tell anyone. Ever. Promise me, Claire. It was totally nothing. I don't even know why I said anything. If you tell, I will totally tell everyone about your secret crush on Jack Messier. Oh my God. You know I didn't mean it, right?"

She's a liar, too. And obviously not the best friend in the world.

She pretends that she and Ben have a future. That he's just confused and that she'll change him. Somehow, he'll fall in love with her eventually. If she could just be a little more perfect than she already is. He'll fall in love with her, and they'll get married and have cute babies and live in a pretty house and drive a stylish car and have real parties with real people and both of them will be there. For real. Not hiding with a boy named Stephen. The one he really loves.

Sammy would write about Grace, most likely. About how they're best friends and how Sammy worries about her. She would also design a food chart to keep track of her intake and—gross—probably her output, too. Sammy and her salads. Sometimes when she's feeling extra fat, she even eats the lettuce plain. I really worry about Sammy. Why do people want to be so skinny? What do they think will happen when they reach their size-zero goal? What happens at zero? Zero means there's nothing left. Why does she want to disappear?

But I know there's more to Sammy than food charts. Sometimes I see her looking out the car window in that *Please get me out of here* way that I feel. But she was never stupid enough to say it out loud like me. Maybe she would write ideas for new cheers for the squad. Maybe she secretly wants to be a dancer. Or a writer. Maybe she hates cheerleading. I don't know.

Lacy might write about her new spot on the cheerleading squad. Her new status as one of the girls. How she wonders if she only made it on cheerleading because she's "solid." That's Grace's code word for fat. But Lacy isn't fat. Just . . . well, it's true. She's solid. She isn't *zero*.

Every cheer squad needs someone who can be their base. Stand at the bottom of the pyramid. Throw the zeros up in the air and catch them. I bet Lacy would write about how that feels. About how Grace convinced her to be on the squad so she could hold them all up. About how she wishes she could look like Grace or Sammy (or me) just one day. About how she is really tired of salads and fat-free ranch dressing, too. And how all of this brings her to wondering why the girls want to be friends with her in the first place. Maybe she'd secretly write that her biggest worry is whether the only reason she is one of the girls is because one of the girls is in love with her brother, who might very well be in love with a boy.

But I don't know that, either.

And this is the problem.

I don't know the real thoughts of my closest friends. I used to, when we were younger. We used to share our dreams. What we wanted to *be* when we grew up. What we *cared* about. I don't know when that stopped. I don't know when finding Grace's boyfriend's parties became more important than trying to find ourselves.

Maybe it's because we became afraid of what we'd find.

What if all there is to this life is this? Is boredom?

If I was a food, I would be plain yogurt. Colorless and a little sour. Is that really worth finding?

My parents are more or less happily married. They have steady, dependable jobs. I don't have a sibling to fight with or make me feel less loved. I have a safe crush on a quiet boy who probably doesn't know I exist. I can write his name next to mine in an old diary, Jack Messier, with hearts all around it, and leave it unlocked in my underwear drawer without worrying anyone will see it because my parents would never try. It is the one and only secret I keep from them. From everyone (except Grace, who somehow figured it out). That, and I've never even kissed a boy. My parents have nothing to worry about.

We live in a medium-size house—not too lavish but not too small, either. My parents never fight. In fact, even when they start to argue about something as mundane as which movie to watch, they fail, because they have the same tastes. They don't argue about politics because they're in the same party. How can you get passionate about something when the other person just says, "I know! I know! Right?"

It's not that I want a tragic life. I'm lucky I have nothing to worry about. Nothing.

And that is what I feel.

I bought this journal because it seemed like writing something down, anything, would be a way to be heard and not silenced.

What do you even mean, Claire?

The problem is, I don't know what I want people to hear. Maybe I just want them to know I'm here. Waiting. Ready to be . . . something. To know, for whatever reason, I matter.

Maybe I just need to be able to feel the significance of my own existence.

I sip my bitter latte and draw a squiggle line across the top of the page in my journal. As I watch the line run across the page, it reminds me of a life line on a heart monitor machine like in the movies. I imagine the little blip in my head as I make the line go up and down until it reaches three-quarters across the page when I decide to flatline it.

Beeeeeeeeeeen

Lifeless.

I look around to see if anyone noticed what I just wrote. No one did.

People continue to talk and type and sip and clink their cups in their saucers. The tiny bells attached to the door of the café jingle, and an attractive couple strolls in, arm in arm. They gesture to Barista Boy and point to a medium-size display cup on the counter.

"Cappuccinos!" the man says strangely and way too loudly.

Barista Boy nods and gets to work, grooving confidently to the music as he makes their drinks. He has such style. Even the frothy sound of the machine makes me feel like I'm in a sophisticated place.

The couple smiles at each other as they walk toward

me with their drinks and sit nearby. The way they smile, I can tell they're in love. They look at each other as if they're glad of the other's existence. Like neither one of them believes their luck.

The woman sits with her back to me while the man sits at a slight angle, so his knees can touch the woman's, which are bare because she's wearing a short and stylish-looking skirt and tall leather boots.

The man reaches for one of her pointy knees. His fingers flex as he squeezes, then lets go. I look down into my coffee cup, no longer steaming. At the line on my notepad. Flatlining.

I take another sip of bitterness.

Even though I've only had a small amount of caffeine, I can feel it entering my veins and making my stomach feel queasy.

The couple settles their things, then the man begins to motion to the woman with his hands. She motions back. I've never seen anyone use sign language in real life. Only on TV. I watch them closely, not realizing I'm staring. But I can't help it. No one ever told me how beautiful signing is. How graceful. How—to ignorant people like me—private.

Their fingers move elegantly, waltzing back and forth as if teeny little people are doing some sort of complex modern interpretive dance, bowing then swinging and dipping, faster and faster. Beautiful in their deliberateness.

I watch, fascinated. Mesmerized.

Jealous.

They continue on, only stopping to take a sip of their cappuccinos. Or to reach forward to touch each other. On the cheek. The hand. The knee again.

I ignore the empty notebook in front of me. The flatline noise gone silent and unplugged. Dead and forgotten.

I'm in such a trance that when the hands stop, I seem to be on pause myself, waiting for their next move. All this time, I haven't been looking at the couple's faces. Just their hands.

But now there's only one hand in view.

And one finger.

Sticking straight and deliberately up and directed at me. The one sign I know. Ugly and angry.

A rush of heat surges through my chest. I can hear the heart monitor on the page beeping again. It ricochets off my ribs as my heart races and blood rushes to my hot, mortified face.

I move my eyes away from the no longer beautiful, elegant finger and to the man's face.

He scowls and makes a sign at me. "Mind your own business!" he shouts.

And I'm finally filled with a feeling.

Shame.

Other people in the cafe look at me now. They look with disdain. Like I'm a terrible, insensitive person. A gawker. A creeper. A voyeur. A loser.

"I'm sorry," I say. "I didn't mean to—"

I cup my hand over my mouth. He can't hear me. God. I am a horrible person.

I wave apologetically the way you might when you cut someone off in traffic by mistake and try to acknowledge that it's your fault. I try to make my eyes look sorry, too. Anything.

But the damage is done.

The man waves back dismissively and inches closer to the woman so I can't see his hands.

The feeling rushing through my veins slows and turns to something thick and heavy. Something that makes me sink in my seat in disgrace.

I close my empty journal and bring my cup to the rubber bin next to the bar. Barista Boy smiles at me but not in the *Hi again, cutie,* kind of way he might have before witnessing what a jerk I am. More like a *poor clueless kid* kind of way. Like he feels sorry for me for being so uneducated. So *not* an insider at this café.

I feel the disapproving eyes of the other customers on me, but especially of the couple. This place will never be my place. These will never be my people. We'll never swap books or talk politics or suggest obscure movies to one another.

As I walk out, I can feel the quiet, glad hands behind me.

I imagine them silently clapping.

III.

Outside, I stand in front of the café, not sure if I should turn left and go home or turn right and wander aimlessly. A city bus drives past and pulls over up ahead. The doors fold open, and a small group of girls steps off. They're wearing school uniforms. They giggle together as they make their way toward me and into the café.

I imagine them taking my table near the graceful-hands couple, too busy chatting and giggling to notice the silent tiny dancers. Maybe the man will watch them, their mouths bouncing soundless words back and forth at one another. Their hands waving meaninglessly to accentuate the words he can't hear. Maybe he will smile inside his own world, glad he can't hear their high pitched chattering. Maybe he'll turn to the beautiful woman across from him and reach for her word-filled hands. Maybe he'll hold them still in his and say how much he loves her with nothing but his light-brown eyes. She'll see the story— their story—unfolding in front of her just by looking at his face.

Why?

Why am I so good at romancing everyone's story but my own?

I wish I could feel the words to my own story start to unfold in my brain, down my arm, and into my fingers. I see, again, the man's middle finger pointed at me, challenging me. *Get your own life.* If only I knew how.

The tips of my fingers do not tingle with the words waiting to be written in my spiral notebook, the way I had imagined they would. There is no café of my dreams, with a clever name on a beautifully painted wooden sign that appears like a beacon, a guiding light in the gray that is my life. It's as if my brand-new blue Sharpie is out of ink before it can write a single word. All I see is a dirty old city street stretched out before me. Endless and promise-less.

And then I'm falling.

My hands hit the pavement first, then my knees. It doesn't hurt so much physically as it does emotionally

Even the sidewalk resents me.

I stand up, cheeks burning, and brush myself off.

My eyes begin to water and it's sort of a relief. I want to cry. I *need* to cry. I look around to see if anyone would notice or care.

A woman with a dog is leaning against the building next to me. The dog, a small one, stands at her side, wagging what should be a tail but is only a stump.

"You tripped over my cane," the woman points out. "Sorry about that. Are you all right?"

"Ye-eah," I say. My hands sting but they're not even scraped, really.

There's a cardboard sign leaning next to the woman.

HOMELESS PLEASE HELP

"Your head was in the clouds like everyone else's," the woman tells me.

Everyone else. Just like everyone else.

"I'm not," I say.

"Huh?"

"Like everyone else." I'm getting used to this lying thing.

She shrugs.

I reach into my purse and fish out my wallet. I don't have much. A five and a few ones. (And the twenty hidden in another compartment for emergencies only.) I decide to go for the five.

"Here," I say, handing it to the woman.

"Big spender!" she says, taking it without resistance.

The dog stays put but continues to wag its stubby tail. He's a wiry-haired thing, with scruffy tufts around his eyes that look like enormous eyebrows.

"Can I pet your dog?" I ask.

My parents have warned me a million times not to talk to strangers. Not to approach dogs I don't know. They've told me about people pretending to be homeless and conning them out of money. I've always been careful. Always crossed the street when I see a person asking for spare change. But here I am, asking to pet this woman's dog, despite the sign that makes it very clear she is homeless.

Maybe that's the problem. I've always been careful.

For what?

I bend down and reach my hand out to the dog. He sniffs it. His tail stub wags so hard and so fast, his rump waddles. I brush my hand softly along his back. The bones of his spine stick out of his fur.

"He's so skinny," I say.

"He's a street dog!" the woman yells. "What do you expect?"

I step back, surprised. She seemed so nice seconds ago.

The dog yips and comes closer to me for more pats.

"I think he needs some food," I say. The more I pet him, the more I think he might be starving.

"Do I look like I have food for him?" the woman asks, all sarcastic.

"You've got five dollars," I point out.

The dog licks my hand. Tastes it. It hurts my heart.

The woman grunts. "There's a bodega on the corner. If you really care, here. Take it and go buy him something." Her voice softens guiltily. "My legs don't want to move just now."

I take the money back. The dog looks up at me with hopeful eyes.

"I'll be right back," I tell him. "What's his name?"

"Oliver."

"I'll be back, Oliver."

He stands on his back legs and holds his front paws bent, as if to beg.

It's the saddest thing I've ever seen.

I hurry to the corner and spot the bodega. Inside, it

smells like tobacco and spices I don't recognize and sour milk. The man behind the counter looks me up and down like I'm something to eat. It's way more disgusting than when Oliver did it.

I ignore him and explore the two small aisles, looking for dog food, but they don't seem to carry any. Instead, I find some cheese and crackers and a bucket of Slim Jims. I'm sure Oliver will like those.

The man at the register looks at my purchase: a box of Triscuits, a packet of Kraft cheese slices, and three Slim Jims.

He rings me up.

"'At'll be seven forty-three," he says.

I give him the five and dig in my purse for the rest.

He puts everything in a flimsy plastic bag.

"Have a nice day!" he says, then spits something brown into a paper cup with blue flowers on it. I can see this is not the first spit, as there's about an inch and a half of disgusting brown liquid already in the cup.

"Thanks," I say, trying not to gag.

I step outside and breathe in the city air thankfully. I don't think it ever smelled less polluted. I rush up the street to Oliver. The plastic bag rustles with each hurried step. When he sees me, Oliver hops up and barks and wags that crazy tail stump. He does his circus act.

I finally know what it means when people say their heart melted.

"What did you get him?" the woman asks. She's sitting now, leaning against the brick wall of the building.

"Just some snacks," I say. I reach in the bag and pull out a Slim Jim. Oliver goes nuts, somehow knowing the treat's for him.

"Be patient," I say as I struggle with the plastic wrapping.

"Would you like one?" I ask the woman. "I bought a few."

She scrunches up her face in disgust. "That's nasty."

"I also bought cheese and crackers," I say. I realize with shame that I asked for the dog's name but not hers.

"I'm Claire," I say. I can hear my parents' collective gasp in my head. "What's yours?"

"Ginny. Short for Virginia."

"That's pretty."

She shrugs like it makes no difference.

I finally manage to peel back the plastic from the admittedly nasty-looking meat product and hold it up to Oliver.

"Sit," I say.

Instead he does his practiced begging pose again.

"OK," I say. "It's true, that's more impressive." I hold

out the meat, and he takes it gently but quickly, then whips it around as he chews

Next I open the box of Triscuits. I hold it out for Ginny first, but she turns it down.

"I don't need that," she says. "Or the dog."

"What do you mean?"

"He's not mine. He likes you. Take him."

"He's . . . not yours?"

"He just started following me, pathetic thing. Street dogs are all around, ya know. But most are smart enough to be more sly. This thing was as bold as you please first time he found me in that alley off Sykes Avenue. That's where the best restaurant Dumpsters are, and the street dogs know it."

I nod, as if I know it too.

"Most dogs cower when a person comes near 'cause they know street people will fight 'em for a good piece of meat or something. They're used to dodging kicks. But this one sauntered right over to me and did his little beggar routine. I didn't give him anything, mind, but he followed me anyway. He's been following me for three days, and I haven't given him a bite."

"Poor thing," I say.

"He's just a dog."

I look down at Ginny. She's wrapped in an old army-green sleeping bag. Her brownish-gray hair is greasy and matted. Her teeth are dirty. Her hands are nearly black with grime. But I act like I care more about her dog than I do her.

What is wrong with me?

"I'm sorry," I say. For the second time today, I am full of shame. This time, it's even worse.

Ginny shrugs again. "Dogs are a lot easier to love than people. You should take him. He doesn't belong on the streets. Miracle he's alive at all."

"But—" I look back and forth from one to the other. There seems to be more to their relationship than three days.

"How did you know his name is Oliver?" I ask suspiciously.

"He had to have a name, didn't he!" she yells, angry again. She pulls the sleeping bag tighter over her shoulders. Oliver walks in circles nervously. I wait, not sure what I'm supposed to do next.

"He made me think of the story of Oliver Twist," Ginny says quietly. "You know. The Dickens story? About the orphan boy. My mother read that to me when I was a little girl. There was a movie, too, but the book was better. This dog reminded me of Oliver because he isn't like all the other street kids. He's . . . special, I think. He should have a real home."

Oliver stops circling and moves closer to Ginny. He sniffs her sleeping bag and wags his tail stump. I think he can sense her sadness. I'm sure he's been with her for longer than she says. But how much longer can he survive without food? Before he gets some disease or nabbed by animal control and put to sleep? Or bitten by another street dog?

Oliver tries to climb onto the sleeping bag. I can smell it from here. Pee and sweat. Ginny nudges him off. "Go on," she says. "Take him. Bring him to a vet. He probably has fleas and tapeworm and who knows what else. But you look like you come from a family that can afford to fix him up."

"Won't you miss him?" I ask.

"I said take him!" she barks. Her face contorts and looks vicious.

Oliver whimpers and cowers, his backside hunched, as if he's trying to tuck his tail between his legs, only the stub isn't long enough.

The sleeping bag comes alive and pushes Oliver away again.

"Do . . . do you want to come home with me?" I ask him.

He inches closer to me and sniffs my shoe.

"Go on!" Ginny growls. Red splotches like fine paint splashes have sprouted on her cheeks and forehead. Her eyes have gone mean.

"But—" I try.

"I said I don't want him!" She starts rocking back and forth inside her bag.

I bend down and put the box of crackers and a packet of cheese next to her. She swipes them up and clutches them to her chest.

"The five bucks would've been better," she mumbles.

"Sorry."

"Just go before I change my mind." Her voice softens. "Take good care of him."

"I will." I wait to see if she wants to say good-bye to her dog. At least give him a pat. But she pulls the sleeping bag up over her shoulders and hides the food inside. Then she pulls the bag all the way over her head and retreats inside completely.

The sleeping-bag body goes still.

Oliver whimpers. We wait together but nothing happens. As I stand there, a feeling creeps up through my feet, my stomach. My heart. I don't know why I'm crying. Oliver looks up at me and wags his stump tail slowly. Sadly.

"Are you OK, miss?" a woman asks. She's holding a little kid's hand.

"Fine," I say. I wipe my eyes. The woman walks on. The kid looks back and waves.

I wait a few more minutes to see if Ginny will come out again, but she doesn't.

I reach inside my bag and pull out my journal and new Sharpie pen. I open the book to the page that has the date. And my flatline. I think about how dead I felt less than an hour ago and how awake I feel now, even though it hurts.

Under the flatline, I leave a note.

I'll take good care of him.

I look at the flatline one more time, then find the twenty hidden in my wallet. I bookmark the page with the bill, then quietly close the book and put it and the pen beside the still sleeping bag.

At the sound of the journal touching the sidewalk, Ginny pokes her head out just a little and looks to see what I put down. She makes a displeased face and hides back in the bag.

Oliver sniffs the bag one more time, then yips, loud and demanding.

Slowly, a filthy hand reaches out of the opening of the bag. And gives me the finger.

No one has ever given me the finger before, and here I am getting it twice in one day. I don't know what that says about me. But I feel like I've deserved it.

At least it makes walking away a bit easier.

Maybe Ginny knows that.

Oliver wags his tail stub and slowly follows, only stopping a few times to whimper and look back at the sleeping bag that is hiding Ginny—a life—completely from the outside world. She has started rocking again. And now, I fear, sobbing.

We stop at the corner one more time to turn back. The bag looks small from here. From here, you can't tell a person is inside. It looks like a pile of garbage someone left on the street.

Oliver sniffs the air.

"You can go back," I tell him.

But he stays.

"Well, then, we have a long walk, my friend, because I'm pretty sure they won't let you on the city bus. Probably not even a taxi."

He yips happily and walks on.

IV.

Oliver stops at each block to wait for the white man-shaped image to appear on the walk sign before crossing. Every so often, he brushes against my leg, and I bend down to give him a pat. My hands smell terrible from his stinky fur, but I don't mind. When we pass a shop owner watering flowers in a window box, I ask if Oliver can have a drink. I look at the water longingly and also regrettably, as it is making me need to pee. I realize I had that stupid coffee drink and forgot to use the bathroom before I left the café. No way can I hold it until we get home.

We.

I smile.

When Oliver has his fill of water, we carry on. Finally, we come to a park where people walk their dogs, jog, and sit on benches to eat during their lunch breaks.

"Should we go in?" I ask.

Oliver shakes and yips. I remember there are porta-potties somewhere near here, so we wander around until we find them.

I hesitate. Will Oliver wait outside for me?

"I've gotta go in there for just a sec," I tell him. I lean

down and scratch behind an ear. "Then we'll go home. OK, boy?"

He barks. It's not a happy bark. It sounds more like a *Don't leave me* one.

I step toward the unoccupied cube on the end. "I'll be right out," I say reassuringly.

Oliver tilts his head, then growls low.

I open the door and he trots over, frantically rubbing his side against my legs. Then he hops into the foul little room.

"Um," I say.

He barks again.

I sigh and join him. It smells terrible inside and I pee as quickly as possible while Oliver waits, watching.

Hovering over the black toilet seat in front of a strange little dog in a disgusting city porta-potty, I start to giggle. When I decided to let the bus take me somewhere, this is the last place I thought I'd end up. Oliver pants and turns in a tight circle, poor thing. I quickly finish and we step outside into the glorious city air.

We walk through the park and are about to exit at the other end when someone with a huge long-haired dog on a leash comes toward us. The dog strains against its red leash and barks at Oliver, who gets low to the ground between me and the other dog and growls. His wire hair stands straight up all the way down his back. His mouth pulls away from his tooth viciously. I realize I should have him on a leash and quickly crouch down to hold him, but he doesn't even have a collar and I don't have anything to hold on to except his scrawny body. I wrap my arms around him protectively and feel how truly skinny he is. He's trembling. I hold tighter.

The other owner struggles as his dog pulls against the leash, clearly intent on tearing Oliver to bits. I hold Oliver tight and wait until the man and his dog pass.

"That's what leashes are for!" the man yells over his shoulder.

He stomps off angrily, and I give Oliver another reassuring squeeze.

"Don't pay attention to him," I say. I carry him a whole block before he finally stops trembling. We stop and I set him down and unwrap another Slim Jim for him.

I squint up toward the street. My house isn't too far now. My parents won't be home, though. I imagine bringing Oliver inside and feeding him something nutritious. Maybe I'll make him a hamburger. Then I'll fill the kitchen sink with warm sudsy water and give him a nice bath. Maybe I'll find a big box in the basement and decorate the outside like a present to put

Oliver in and surprise my parents. I know they'll freak out at first, but I also know they'll love him. Just like I already do. I'll let him nap on the couch and get some rest, then I'll take him for another walk and show him the neighborhood.

I can't remember the last time I looked forward to the rest of the day. I've forgotten about the girls and the game I'm missing tonight. And the homework I forgot to bring home. And to feel bad about the usual messages I haven't received since I lost my part-of-the-girls status.

For the first time, I don't feel like everyone else.

I feel like me.

This is *me*.

"Ready, boy?" I ask when Oliver finishes his Slim Jim.

He wags his bum happily.

As we walk toward home, I realize I also forgot about finding a new trendy café and whatever it was I dreamed of writing. I forgot all about the man with his finger, and how he made me feel. Like a fake. A fraud.

My café fantasy was just that. A dumb dream. But this moment, this walking home with a new friend, is real. Is true. Is what I was looking for. That something more to life I've always wanted.

Something to care about.

I walk faster. Oliver starts to run ahead, so I jog after him. He yips at me in a friendly way, like, *I don't know where we're going, but I can't wait to get there!*

"Faster!" I yell, and sprint past him.

He yips again, and we charge ahead.

THREE:
IT'S
TEMPORARY
(Dewey: 10:37 a.m.)

I.

EVERY MORNING AT APPROXIMATELY 7:25, I pull out of my driveway and head to hell, also known as Little Cindy's restaurant. I don't like to talk about work. It's temporary. My dad's going to get me a real job at the Ford dealership he works at as soon as I turn twenty-one. Two years seems like forever. But this situation is temporary.

At approximately 7:33, I reach my first traffic light. I always gaze at the green house on the corner and remember the girl who used to live there. Her name was Marcie. She was hot. Long dark hair. Huge tits. Tight jeans. Leather boots. She never looked at me. I heard she went to New York and became a model.

Everyone I graduated with last year seems to have gone off somewhere to become something.

Except me.

At approximately 7:42, I drive past my old high school. I roll down my window, stick out my hand, and give it and everyone inside the finger. Sometimes there are still late arrivals rushing through the parking lot to get to school. I always hope they'll see me, but they never do.

Sometimes when I stick out my finger, a car behind me honks. Sometimes with approval. Sometimes not. It makes no difference to me.

At approximately 7:53, I obey the ENTER HERE sign in the parking lot and park in the farthest corner. I sit in my car and breathe. A lot. I hate my job. My father always says beggars can't be choosers. He says that someday I'll be glad I had the experience. I'll appreciate what I have more.

My dad is kind of like my dad and kind of like my best friend. We do a lot together. We lift weights at the gym. We wash his car and my car. We keep the yard up nice. We watch TV. It's always been like that since my mother dumped us.

That's another thing I don't like to talk about.

I guess you could call what I do before I go inside "car meditation." If I don't do some serious controlled breathing and positive visualization (me, not at this job), I'll lose it. I will do something I will regret.

I am not a patient person. I am not a *tolerant* person. That's what they told me at school. In mediation every time I got in a fight.

You need to be more tolerant, Dewey. Do you know what that means?

I see myself sitting at a conference table being talked at. My arms are crossed. I'm wearing a black T-shirt. My hands are curled around my biceps. I flex them and feel the muscles tighten. Back then, I thought I was pretty strong. I had no idea what my full potential was. I like to imagine *that* me in the body of *this* me jumping across the table and punching the principal in the face.

Are you listening, Dewey? Do you have anything to say?

I did, but I never bothered to share. No one would believe me anyway.

Loser. That's what Mr. Weidenheff used to call me. I'd stare at the stupid motivational posters on the wall telling me to BE A READER because IT WILL TAKE YOU ANYWHERE and wonder who they were supposed to inspire. Not me, that's for sure.

Why don't you just quit school now? You'll never amount to anything.

That's what he liked to say to the non-college-track

kids. It wasn't just me. I think telling us we were losers made him feel tough. I showed him what tough is.

It's wrong to punch your teacher. You could get expelled. So I ended up punching a lot of other poor assholes instead.

There was a lot of crap about breathing slowly. Counting backward. Removing yourself from the situation. Staying away from people who cause you to have strong feelings. Like I had a choice.

No one knew about the Heff's secret messages to me and the other losers. Unless you count the janitor, who one time was cleaning in the hallway after the Heff kept me late. When I came out of the room, he muttered "asshole" under his breath. I choose to believe he was talking about the Heff and not me. But the janitor wasn't going to help me. No one was.

The principal and the counselors didn't know I couldn't stay away from the person who caused me to have strong feelings because he was my teacher.

But then my teacher shot himself in the head.

Sometimes I wonder if it was the losers like me who pushed him over the edge. But then I force myself not to think about it.

Instead, I practice keeping my cool.

Remember to breathe.

Count backward.

Remove myself from the situation.

Stay away from people who cause me to have strong feelings.

For the most part, this is easy. Except when I get to work. And except when I see our dickhead next-door neighbor boy, who doesn't lift a finger to do the yard work their house desperately needs. All the houses on our street are neat and tidy. All but the damned house next door. The mom works all the time, and the two kids don't do crap to help out. I don't know where their father is. Every Saturday, instead of going outside to mow their lawn or trim their hedges, the little bitch boy races out the door and jumps in his friend's car to go waste time all day doing who knows what. Sometimes I want to kill him.

The sister is no better. She does the same thing. Always going off with her friends. At least she's hot and likes to give me a show when she walks down their front steps. Shaking her ass when she sees me watching. Slut.

Breathe.

Sometimes, on the weekends when the brats are off with their friends, I see the mom carrying stuff from her car into the house. Once she left the front door open, and I saw inside the front hall. It was filled with boxes and trash bags all the way to the ceiling. When she caught me looking, she slammed the door like *I* was the weirdo.

Count backward. Ten. *Breathe.* Nine. *Breathe.* Eight. *Breathe.* Seven. *Breathe.* Six. *Breathe.* Five. *Breathe.* Four. *Breathe.* Three. *Breathe.* Two. *Breathe.* One. *Breathe.*

At approximately 7:55, I get out of my car. I hold my breath, knowing what's coming. When I can't hold it any longer, I relent and try not to gag on the greasy restaurant smell waiting to violate my lungs. I fight the urge to puke.

I press the lock button on my key chain. The car chirps good-bye. I admire the shine my dad and I gave it the night before.

Be back soon, I say in my head.

I'll be right here, it replies reassuringly.

I say the chant inside my head with every step toward hell. There are thirty-two.

It's temporary. It's temporary.

At approximately 7:59, I get my time card and slide it in the slot.

Punch.

Clocked in.

I hear Mr. Weidenheff's voice:

You'll never amount to anything.

And wish I could remove myself from the situation.

I put on the finishing touches of my uniform. My name tag. Gold. Because I'm the manager. My hat. Black. Like everyone else's. My earpiece. A contraption I use to boss everyone around.

No one will greet me as they file up to get their cards and punch in. I'm not a good coworker. I'm orderly. I like to run a clean ship. I don't put up with lazy asses, ex-cons, old people who don't have the energy for this job but don't have enough money to retire, teen moms, or stoners.

Unfortunately, these are the most common types of people attracted to this job. Then there's me. There's a reason I got promoted to manager in less than six months. Mainly it's because most people quit within two.

At approximately 8:02, I check the schedule and make a note of who I'll be supervising at the counter. Alice, Kristen, and Jeff.

Alice is like seventy-two years old and needs retraining every day because she forgets everything she learned the day before. I should have recommended that we fire her by now, but she makes me cookies sometimes and I like that.

Kristen is young. Pretty cute. Nice hair. Dropped out of school last year because she got pregnant. We went to the same school, but I don't remember her. Her crowd didn't go near my crowd. Now she works here to support her kid. I'm guessing that kid doesn't eat well.

Jeff falls under the stoner category. I don't like his attitude. He thinks everything is funny. He doesn't care when I yell at him. Or tell him he's working too slowly. Too sloppily. Too inefficiently.

You're so intense, man.

That's true. I am intense.

At approximately 8:06, we deal with the breakfast rush and the smell of egg and chicken. Hell is hot and smells like chicken eggs and chicken meat because some crazy bastards eat chicken on a biscuit for breakfast. These people are on the list of people I fantasize about pushing over a cliff.

Now it's 10:37.

Everything has gone as previously described. No surprise.

92

I expect the rest of the day to go just as predictably as it does every day. The breakfast smells have started to fade as the cooks in the back start to prep for lunch. It still smells like chicken in grease. But now there's beef in grease mixed in. If it weren't for the French fries helping to lessen the stench, I don't think I would survive. Alice carefully wipes the counters while Kristen follows with a dry cloth. Jeff wanders aimlessly, trying to look busy. I check supplies throughout.

Napkins. Check.

Straws. Check.

Ketchup and other condiments. Check.

Still hate my job. Check.

11:05.

The lunch crowd starts to flow in. It's quiet at first, with mostly old people who eat early. But by noon there will be a line, and I will have to make sure everything stays orderly. I especially have to make sure that Alice doesn't waste time chatting up all her old friends. Everyone seems to love her, and they have no problem telling her how sad it is to see her behind the counter. They don't care how that might make everyone on this side of the counter feel.

Sometimes I imagine myself saying something to

the old man who clearly has a thing for Alice, though sometimes I see him checking out Kristen. The dirty bastard. He's always telling Alice how hard it is to see her working. I want to tell him how sad it is to see him eating lunch at a freakin' Little Cindy's every goddamned day. Doesn't he get how sad *that* is?

No.

Probably not.

At least he's still on the right side of the counter.

12:05.

Things are in full swing. I bark orders at everyone and march around behind the counter, helping the cashiers put the right food on the right trays. Every seven minutes I swivel around and go back to the kitchen to yell at Simon, the burger guy, to keep the burgers flipping. He's friends with Jeff. He dances in place as he stares at the grill. God. What is it with stoners? They're always so goddamned happy.

"Simon!" I yell, just to harsh his mellow.

Sometimes, I admit, I can be a bastard, too.

He looks up and shakes his head, then goes back to flipping. I would fire him, but I haven't had any applications in two weeks. At least not any that are worth considering.

Every so often I go out to the dining area to make sure

there aren't any spills I missed or trash on the floor. I use this as an excuse to check on my car through the window. It's an electric-blue 1988 Ford Mustang convertible that my dad helped me buy. When it came in at the dealership, he knew it was the perfect car for us to fix up together. A classic. I spend about as many hours working on that car as I do at this place. I know that sounds pathetic. It is. But that's what happens when you barely graduate from a crap school and have zero interest in college and are destined to amount to nothing.

When my dad and I get home from work, we buff the car. We rake or mow the lawn, depending on what the yard needs. We clean the house. We both like order. Unlike our goddamned next-door neighbors, the slobs. I bet they don't even own a lawn mower. I offered to mow their place for them, cheap, but they said no. Or, I should say, the freaky mom said no. I wanted to tell her that maybe her two kids should get off their asses and do some work around the house like I do. But I just smiled in an obnoxious way to make her feel bad.

I really can be a bastard sometimes.

But that damn house drives me crazy.

They drive me crazy.

If it weren't for the girl giving me the occasional strut, I'd be tempted to set the place on fire.

She's a cheerleader. Did I mention that? She has long dark hair. An amazing body. She knows it, too. Just like Marcie. She shakes her ass extra hard when she sees me outside. She likes it when I watch. Marcie did, too. I could see it made her feel powerful. But I wasn't allowed to get too close. I wasn't good enough for anything more than watching from a safe distance.

I hate teases.

But I still watch.

Whenever her brother catches me, I can tell he's going nuts, which I love. Skinny little turd wouldn't dream of coming after me except in his fantasies. He knows this. I know it. She knows it. It's a game we play.

12:20.

I am back to pacing behind the counter. Bored. But then a nice surprise. The little turd from next door comes in with all his turd friends. Most people from the high school use the drive-thru. They don't have time to eat inside during lunch period. I wait for him and gesture for Kristen to step aside. I got this.

He looks at me. I look at him. I can tell he's nervous. He took a paver from our driveway just to be an asshole, and I've been waiting for a chance to scare the crap out of him ever since. Why take a brick from someone's drive-way? Don't they have enough crap in that house? Is that what they do? Go around taking things from everyone in the neighborhood? Or is it just us?

My dad already replaced it. But I know what thin little punk tried to do. Trying to piss me off like our neat yard is just a joke to him. He thinks he's so funny. Well, I can take something from him, too. I smile, take his money, and tell him the last thing he wants to hear. About me and his slutty tease sister. It's not clear from his expression if he really believes me, but it doesn't matter.

Mission accomplished.

Prick.

II.

2:00.

The lunch rush has died down, and I get to take my break. I get thirty minutes. I savor it.

Soon the assholes from the high school will show up again like they own the place. They'll look at me and not look at me. They'll see some schmuck. That's all. Not a particular one. Just one of *those* guys. One of those losers who didn't go to college. Didn't get a real job. Didn't get a life. They'll wonder if I ever even graduated. I flex my biceps and wonder what it would feel like to hurt them.

It's temporary.

In two years, I'll be twenty-one, and I'll quit this job faster than . . . I don't know. Just fast. Faster than my Mustang at zero to sixty. I'll go work with my dad and earn commissions, and we'll shoot to the top of the sales board. Unstoppable. I'll buy my own place. And people like Marcie and that slutty little tease neighbor will *wish* I'd do more than check them out.

Maybe my mother will find out about us and maybe she'll regret leaving. Too bad for her. It will be way too late to come crawling back.

I take my breaks outside. I bring my own lunch. No way am I going to eat this stuff and gain a thousand pounds like that guy who ate at McDonald's every day and made a movie about it and almost died. It's bad enough I have tons of acne from sneaking the occasional fry.

No.

I sit at one of the picnic tables near my car.

Hi, I say to it inside my head.

Hey, dude, it says back.

I would sit *in* my car, but my work clothes smell like fried meat and I don't want my car to smell like that. Instead, I look out beyond the parking lot and pretend I'm a customer. Pretend I'm here from my real job, on lunch break. I eat a turkey sandwich and drink a protein shake.

Slowly.

I might know the number of bites it takes to finish the sandwich. *Nineteen.*

I might know how many swallows it takes to finish my protein shake. *Twenty-one.*

I might know how many pieces of orange peel I have to break off before I finish peeling. *Six.*

2:27.

I wipe my mouth with a napkin and throw my trash away. I take slow breaths as I walk back to hell.

Five hundred eighty-four work days to go.

2:31.

I watch suspiciously from behind the counter while the high-schoolers file inside and get in line. They do not respect the rules. They snap gum that I will find later pressed under a chair or table. They push each other. They grope each other. They drop trash on the floor.

I hate them all.

I was never like them in school. I didn't get to hang out with my friends. We didn't go anywhere after school together. We had jobs after school. We worked our asses off at crap jobs like this. Got made fun of by assholes like them. Survived. Barely graduated high school. Got slightly less crap jobs. Tried to forget the Marcies and the rest of the people who only let us watch. Drool. Wish we were them. But never let us get too close.

We were outsiders, waiting to become invisible.

Waiting to amount to nothing.

I cross my arms at my chest and flex my muscles again. I like looking threatening. I like looking tough. I realize my cobalt-blue shirt and stiff black baseball cap don't exactly help, but the muscles cancel them out. That's what I pretend.

I go to the gym every day after work. It helps me release my aggression. It also helps me get buff. And I am. I know I said that already. But it's important to me. It's important to me to know with confidence that I could beat the crap out of any one of these privileged jerks.

I stand behind Alice as she takes an order. I make her nervous. Her fingers shake above the keypad. She turns to me and makes an innocent, helpless gesture. What does she want *me* to do?

Kristen moves much more quickly and efficiently. Her fingers dance over the keyboard she's already memorized. She's smart. She shouldn't be here. She should be on the other side of the counter hanging out with her friends, poor fool. Instead she let herself get knocked up, and now she's one of us.

Jeff is laughing. His pothead friends are ordering more food than they can probably afford. I'm sure he'll try to get away with giving them free stuff. But it won't happen. Not while I'm managing. I walk over to him and he straightens up. His friends look at me and burst out laughing.

Go ahead. Laugh. Losers.

Jeff gets all serious and tells them how much they owe. They freak out over the price and have him cancel the order. They get one order of large fries to share. Predictable.

I glance out at the crowd again and spot that little dick from next door. I can't believe he came back. We lock eyes. He looks pissed. Seriously pissed. Good.

I pace back and forth behind the counter, just waiting for him to get to the front of the line. But all of a sudden, the little turd and his friends take off. I see them running in the parking lot. Then there's a commotion at the back of the line. Everyone's gasping and yelling, and some guy is on the floor. I jump over the counter. What the hell is going on?

The guy looks bad. Maybe it's a heart attack. Who knows? Things happen fast and I do what I can to help the poor dude. His wife and kid hang on to him as if he's going to rise up and float away. I can see why. He is not in good shape. He looks like a burned-out business guy. He's wearing a really ugly brown suit, and his shoes have those gross leather tassels on them that were popular in, like, the nineties or something. He looks kind of pathetic to tell the truth, and not just because he's clinging to life. I make a vow on the spot that I will never look like that. Ever.

Everyone stands around. Staring. Waiting to see if the guy will die. The wife and kid look desperate and helpless. I also vow never to look like that. I decide to do what I can and bark some orders. Get the guy some water. Tell everyone to step back and give him some room. What else can I do? I have no idea.

Luckily the EMTs show up in minutes and take over. I walk outside and make sure everything goes smoothly. The fresh air is nice and I drink it in guiltily, knowing I shouldn't allow myself to feel good when some guy is dying in the wailing ambulance that is taking off down the road.

I take a few more deep breaths anyway.

I turn and force myself to walk back to the front door. Sixteen steps.

It's temporary. It's temporary. It's temporary. It's temporary. It's temporary. It's temporary. It's temporary. It's temporary. It's temporary. It's temporary. It's temporary. It's temporary. It's temporary. It's temporary. It's temporary. It's temporary.

In hell, things have gone back to normal.

The crowd has gotten back in line. The registers have started beeping again, and no one would ever know that a guy might have just croaked on the floor we're all standing on.

I think about my own dad and what I would do if something happened to him. But I don't want to imagine that. Because nothing can. Not before this temporary life is over and we live our dream.

III.

4:59.

Alice taps my shoulder. "I'm going to clock out now," she says. Her eyes are kind. For a minute, I feel bad for being such a jerk to her.

"OK," I say. "Have a good night."

The rest of the workers follow. The poor saps on the next shift wait to take their places. They look tired, and they haven't even started yet. I punch my time card and file it in my designated slot. I admit, I smile. At the moment, there is little else that feels better than checking out of this place.

When I step outside, I take off my cap and let the breeze blow over my sweaty head. I open the trunk and rip off my shirt, roll it up in a ball, and stick it in a plastic bag so it won't smell up the car. I put on a tank top for the gym and get in the car.

Breathe.

Five hundred eighty-four days to go.

5:07.

I drive to the gym with the windows down and the radio blasting. When I go past the hospital, I wonder if the guy from earlier made it. I turn the volume up louder. The bass thumps through my chest and makes me feel alive. I rock my head to the beat. This is the happiest part of my day.

5:23.

I think the chick behind the counter at the gym is into me. She always asks to see my club card photo before I go in and then takes an extra long time looking at it, then me, it, then me. Smiling like she wants me.

Supposedly she's dating one of the personal trainers, but I never see her with him.

Today when she takes my card, she spends even more

104

time checking me out. When she hands it back, she licks her lips. I smirk seductively and leave her there.

I head to the locker room, finish changing, and find my dad already lifting weights. We spot each other for the next hour. Then we run side by side on the treadmill. Three miles in twenty-two point five minutes.

After, we sit in the sauna. We don't need to talk. Just sit and sweat whatever we have left out.

We shower.

We go home. He in his Ford Explorer. Me in my Mustang.

When I drive past the school, I flip it the bird again. The car behind me honks. Then I realize it's my dad. He sticks his finger out too. Heh.

At home we walk around the yard before going inside, pulling up any weeds that might have cropped up. My dad carries a bottle of Roundup and sprays. Sometimes a piece of trash blows onto the lawn and we pick up that too. Once, a Little Cindy's burger wrapper blew across the front walkway. I set it on fire.

7:45.

We get dinner together. Salmon. Rice. Broccoli. We always sit in the same place at the table. My dad on one side, me on the other. My mother used to sit on the end, sort of between us. Even though that was a long time ago,

I sometimes wait to start eating until she sits down. When my dad digs in, I remember she's not here anymore.

Tonight I eat my food slowly, around the plate. Bite of salmon. Bite of rice. Bite of broccoli. One at a time, taking turns. My dad likes to take a little bit of each food and put it on his fork so he gets a taste of all three at once. This is one of the only things we don't have in common.

"I saw Rachel checking you out," my dad tells me after he takes a long drink of Bud Light from the beer glass I gave him for Christmas last year. It's a Patriots glass. That's our favorite football team. I take my own drink from my Red Sox glass. That's our favorite baseball team, and the glass I gave my dad the Christmas before. My dad lets me drink beer at dinner just like him, even though I'm only nineteen.

"I doubt it," I say.

"No. She was."

I shrug. "She has a boyfriend."

"She doesn't have a ring yet. Fair game."

"She won't go out with me as long as I'm a fast-food manager."

He sighs and takes another drink. "That's temporary."

I smile. "Maybe her boyfriend will be too. I can wait." That's my plan. I know she's into me now. No doubt. But I'm not letting her know where I work.

My dad nods and takes another bite. The food is carefully balanced in three parts on his fork. Pink, yellow, and green. When he chews, he makes a kind of contented grunting noise. I've caught myself making the same sound on occasion. It used to drive my mother crazy.

Would the two of you shut up, *for Christ's sake! It's like living with animals!*

We made her so miserable.

"By the way, I have a date tomorrow," my dad says. He pulls his phone from his back pocket and brings up a message with a photo, then hands it to me.

The woman looks OK.

"Three left on my plan," he says. "This one seems real nice."

"Yeah," I say. "She looks nice. If it doesn't work, are you gonna renew?"

He shrugs and takes another drink. "Who knows? This whole online dating thing is costing me a fortune. Sometimes I think ladies just sign up for free food. Last week's date ordered a ton of extra food and had the waitress put almost all of it in doggie bags to take home. I bet she's feeding her kids off dates."

"Seriously?"

"Yeah. I think so."

He takes the phone back and sets it on the table.

"I never really dated before. Your mom and I could never afford to go out to eat. Didn't want to. All we wanted to do was find a place we could be alone to—"

"Don't say it," I interrupt. It's hard to imagine my mom and dad being close. All I remember is how much she seemed to hate him. Nothing he did was good enough. Nothing.

My dad says she was sick. Mentally. He finally convinced her that she should see a doctor. She used to do some sort of crazy things that I don't really want to talk about. Most of the scars she left have healed and disappeared. But they're still there inside.

Anyway. She ended up having an affair with her doctor and leaving us for a better life. Her doctor convinced her it wasn't good for her recovery to see us. She agreed.

For a long time, I tried to be better, in case she came back. My dad did too. We picked up the house. We mowed the lawn. We made everything perfect. Kept it perfect. Still do.

Even though we know she's never coming back.

It's a just-in-case thing.

"Well," my dad says, "we'll see what happens."

"Yup," I say.

We finish eating, bring our dishes to the kitchen,

and wash them. Then my dad does what he always does. Opens another beer, pours it into his Patriots glass, and watches *Law and Order* reruns in the living room.

I do what I always do. I go outside to get some air. Seems like I'm always trying to get some air.

IV.

8:32.

It's chilly on the front steps under the light. It's too cold for bugs to swarm the bulb in their frantic way.

Why do they do that, anyway?

I fill my lungs with the biting, sharp night air. Hold it in till it stings, then slowly breathe it out. I do this five times, like always. Then I breathe normal and wait. Wait to be disappointed.

The neighborhood is quiet. I like this time of night when everything's peaceful and orderly. Next door, I realize there's a car parked at the end of the driveway. I squint and try to see what make it is. I see movement inside. Then the door opens and Hot Cheerleader steps out. She's pissed. She starts screaming at whoever's inside the car. Another car pulls up behind them. The lights on the first car come on, and it takes off down the road.

The brother gets out of the second car and runs over to his sister.

"What's all that racket!" I yell, to let them know I'm watching.

They ignore me.

The brother steps closer to her and reaches out in a comforting way. She brushes past before he can touch her. The other car still idles at the curb, headlights interrupting the peaceful dark night.

"Hey! I'm talking to you!" I yell.

The brother waves to whoever's in the car and they drive away. Then the two start to walk toward their house through the jungle of uncut lawn. The girl does not wiggle her hips for me. The boy scowls in my direction.

"Hey!" I call again. I don't even know why.

They both finally stop and look over. Now I have to say something.

"You ever gonna mow that lawn, bitch?" I ask.

"Who are you calling a bitch?" Hot Cheerleader asks.

I smile. They know.

"Leave my brother alone!" she yells. She looks at me like I am dirt.

"You live in a dump!" I call out.

They just laugh.

They laugh!

And then Hot Cheerleader raises her hot arm and gives me the freakin' finger.

Assholes.

Before they go inside, Bitch Boy turns and waves, all friendly. "Good night!"

I shake my head at them.

Idiots.

I open the door and reach inside to turn the light off, then stand on the steps in the dark. It's quiet again. Quiet and peaceful. Next door, the lights come on inside the mess house. The shades are always drawn, but lines of light outline the rectangular windows. I imagine the brother and sister climbing over all their mother's crap to get to their bedrooms. It's a pathetic image, and I turn away and look down the quiet street instead.

Sometimes when I stand out here in the peacefulness, I wonder where my mom is. She was always coming out here to stand in the dark, alone. She never let me stand with her. She had to get away from us.

From our mess. From our smell. From our noise. From our presence. She hated being inside the house. Hated being inside the car. Hated being trapped. With us. She always needed *air*.

When she left, I came out here and stood. I waited and wondered what it was she got out here.

And I wondered if she would come back.

I waited in the dark and hoped. I looked up and down the street, catching my breath every time I saw headlights. But every time, the headlights floated past or turned before they got here. One year. Then two. Then five.

I breathe in deeply again. Feel the familiar sting.

Come back.

I wait.

Our yard is all picked up now. We have nice cars. The house is freshly painted. Everything is in its place. No clutter. I know how to be quiet. I know how to be good.

Come back.

I wait some more.

I wait for the headlights.

I wait for the car, pulling into the driveway.

I wait to see the face I've missed and longed for, even though it hurt me.

Even though she treated me like *nothing*.

I wait.

And wait.

And breathe the air just like she did.

And fear that, maybe, this situation is not temporary after all.

FOUR: BAD BOYS

(Jack: 11:55 a.m.)

I.

CAL, DYLAN, AND I CRAM INTO CAL'S baking-hot Subaru Forester during lunch. Cal bangs his hands against the steering wheel to pound out the rhythm of the music that's blasting through the speakers and making my teeth vibrate. Dylan juts his head out the passenger-side window and pants like a dog thrilled to be going for a ride, except he doesn't actually look very happy. He tries to copy Cal by pounding the dash to the beat, but the glove compartment keeps popping open when he does it, so he finally stops.

Cal's car is kind of falling apart. It's a hand-me-down from Cal's mom and is a total mommy car in every way.

First, it's white. Second, it still has the PROUD PARENT OF AN IRVING MIDDLE SCHOOL HONOR STUDENT bumper sticker on it from three years ago, the last year Cal showed anything resembling promise.

Poor Cal. He's already a year older than us because when he was little his parents read in some child psychology book that they should wait a year to have him start school because it would give him an academic advantage. I guess it did, up to a point. Cal claims the sticker is too old and stuck on and won't come off. But really, I think he's the one who's proud. Lucky for us, an unexpected advantage of Cal being one year older is that he has his license one year sooner. It's probably the one and only thing anyone envies about us.

Whenever we go out with Cal, we sit in the same seats. I am always in the back. I make a point to sit behind the passenger seat so I don't have to see myself in the rearview mirror. I made that mistake once and spent the whole ride being able to see my acne (or, as Dylan would say, my crater face), my bad haircut (or, as Dylan would say, bed head), and, worst of all, my gigantic nose (no one comments on the nose, out of respect for the fact that there's nothing I can do about it). Since then, I've always avoided the Look How Ugly You Are seat. But I'm still in the back. These have been our assigned seats since Cal got his license and the keys to the Great White Beast all in the same day. Damn, his mom is generous. Dylan and I aren't likely to see our first cars until we graduate from college, if we even make it that far.

My parents share one car. It's a silver Prius that sits in the driveway collecting dust like a proud monument to my parents' dedication to Going Green. I mean it just *sits* there. And it's already the greenest car you can get around here. The only time we ever drive the thing is when my parents have to go someplace on business, or if one of us has a doctor's appointment or some other appointment we can't walk, ride bikes, or take the bus to. My parents literally cringe when Cal shows up to get me for school in the Great White. But I continue to point out to them that with three guys in the car, we make a pretty respectable carpool. They just sigh.

Two years ago when they bought my twin sisters a tandem mountain bike, the girls actually burst into tears. "But it will be cute!" my mother insisted. It was not cute. My sisters spent a year hiding the bike in an alleyway on the way to school and hoofing it the rest of the way, to avoid humiliation. No one stole the unlocked bike. No one was surprised.

At the traffic light, Cal rolls the windows down and pumps the volume so the bass changes the rhythm of my heart. *Bam* bam-bam. *Bum* bam-bam. The late-fall air wafts into the car. The smell of dried leaves always reminds me of Halloween for some reason. Walking through neighborhoods with the guys, dressed as hobos, kicking fallen leaves as we trudged along with our pillowcases stuffed with candy. Sometimes I wish we weren't too old to do that anymore.

There's a Ford Taurus next to us. Cal signals for us to check out the driver. He has on a brown suit jacket. His window is down, too, and there's a trickle of sweat dripping from his temple, even though it's kind of cold out. He looks like the kind of guy who always smiles, even if he's just severed a limb. Polite to the point of agony.

I know what that's like, not wanting to make waves. You'd never know it by the guys I hang out with, but I do. I hate conflict. I hate awkward situations. I just want everyone to get along and go with the flow. My mother says she doesn't know how she and my dad could have raised such a passive child. Seriously? She and my dad are so loud and obnoxious, there isn't any room left in the house for my words. My friends think my parents are cool because they're hippie activists. In reality, they're just annoying. I'm not complaining, not really. I'd rather have annoying parents who care about something important than absent parents who don't care at all.

"Get ready," Cal says. It's hard to hear over the music, but we see his lips move and know what's coming.

When the light turns green, Cal guns it and pulls in front of Taurus Man. Then, when we get to the next set of lights, he slams on his brakes. I almost can't hear the tires squeal, the music is so loud. We sort of rock to a stop. Then there's a crunching sound.

Cal turns off the music and looks around, all innocent and fake-confused, like he doesn't know what just happened.

Taurus Man gets out of his car and straightens his tie nervously.

He's a sad sack, that guy. I knew it the moment I saw him. Obviously, so did Cal.

He comes toward the driver's side holding his wallet.

Some cars behind us honk.

The guy's hands are shaking.

"I, uh . . . you stopped kind of suddenly . . . uh . . ."

He fumbles with his wallet.

Cal motions for Dylan to go take a look.

He dashes around the back and inspects, then comes back.

"Bumper's scratched," Dylan says. "Your headlight's broken," he tells the guy.

"Look," the guy says nervously. "I, um, I'm really sorry. But . . . Do you think we could handle this ourselves?"

"Lemme guess," says Cal, all cool. "You don't want to deal with the cops and insurance."

I don't know how Cal gets these guys. How he picks them out. Sometimes it's a lady. Tipsy. Or an old person who can barely see over the steering wheel. It's always the same. Let's take care of this with some cold, hard cash. Fast. No need to involve the cops. Easy money.

I rub my neck on cue. The guy sees me do it. I feel a twinge of guilt. Actually, it's more like a long tight twist in my chest that spreads through my body. I hate this game.

"You OK, son?"

"Yeah, I think so," I say.

Why do I go along with this?

Why.

"I have insurance," he tells us. "But I have this very important job interview. And if we call the police, I could be late. And . . ."

Cal nods patiently.

"Here. This is all I have. I see you boys aren't wearing seat belts."

It's a lame attempt to scare us into not demanding more than he's got. Or to call the cops.

"I'm not even sure that scratch wasn't already there," he adds.

He's probably right. The Great White isn't exactly in pristine condition. But he still forks over some money.

Cal takes the cash and nods at him. "This'll do."

Relief floods the guy's face, and he scurries back to his car. Cal turns the music back up and puts the pedal to the metal even though the light is starting to change.

"Squeeze the freakin' lemon!" Cal yells over the music. The yellow light switches to red just as we pass under it. Cal and Dylan each stick their hands out the window and give the guy the finger. Then Dylan surprises me by leaning his head out the window and yelling, "Suck-ah!" at the guy. I turn and watch the poor man realize what just happened. I imagine him punching the steering wheel as we drive away, leaving him stuck at the red light.

Cal shakes the wad of money like it's a trophy, then hands it to Dylan. Lunch money for the week and beer money for the weekend.

Dylan leans back and smiles, shaking his head and counting out the money. He's been our treasurer since we were in elementary school and formed our secret club in my backyard. We've always pooled our money to buy stuff together. It started with lumber and nails for the tree house we made. Then candy we were forbidden to eat. Fun Dip was the best. We'd see who could eat all the sugar and still end up with the dipping stick at the end. As we got older, we switched to Mountain Dew and energy drinks. We'd see who could drink the most, and then we'd go spastic on our sugar and caffeine highs, racing around the yard. Later, we bought our first pack of cigarettes. Now it's beer. And sometimes weed. Or a juice bottle half filled with liquor from a parent's stash. Over the years, our platform in the tree grew walls, then a roof, then a door with a padlock. And even though it's cramped with the three of us inside, we still meet up there before we go out. To get loaded. To talk. To be those kids we were all those years ago, the Three Musketeers cliché, before we head out and act like the dicks we somehow think we have to be in order to have any fun.

We stop at Little Cindy's and get lunch. Then we cruise through town and wolf down square burgers, filling the car with the smell of French fries and greasy meat. Cal and Dylan discuss whether or not we should cut out for the rest of the day, but, like always, we wind up heading back to school. I don't contribute an opinion on the matter. I never do. I just lean back, look out my window, eat, and enjoy the familiar banter. Sometimes "endure" is more accurate. It depends. Sometimes, I look out my window and think, *There must be more to life.*

But so far I haven't found it.

II.

At school, we pile out of the car, and Cal yells at us for leaving our paper wrappers and ketchup-smeared napkins on the floor. He grabs it all up and shakes the pile of crap at us. "And you guys wonder why my car smells like a Dumpster!"

"It couldn't have anything to do with Dylan's nasty feet?" I ask.

"My feet don't smell!" Dylan whines. "Do they?" He lifts his foot up and bends down to try to get his face close to his ratty sneaker and nearly falls over.

"Pathetic," Cal says, walking ahead.

We follow him, like always.

My next class is English Lit. of the Twentieth Century with Ms. Lindsay. I wanted to take an easy elective, but my parents of course wouldn't let me. I'm pretty sure every straight guy in school is in love with our teacher. She's only in her twenties and totally hot. Well, hot compared to the rest of the teachers, anyway. But no one respects her. The boys make crude noises when she turns her back. The girls all seem to hate her because it's pretty obvious all the single boys lust after her, and they probably suspect that even the boys who have girlfriends fantasize Ms. Lindsay's face on them. It's not her fault she's beautiful. But, I suppose, she could dress a little crappier and not wear so much lipstick or whatever.

The other problem is that she replaced a dead guy. Mr. Weidenheff. He taught here for ages, and then all of a sudden he just went and offed himself at the end of last year. Shot himself in the head. It was kind of insane. Everyone has a different theory for why he did it, but of course no one knows for sure. I had him last year, and I don't remember him seeming depressed. Frustrated, maybe, that none of us seemed to care as deeply about *Moby-Dick* as he did, but honestly, is that a reason to call it quits—permanently?

I can't really imagine what it must be like for poor Ms. Lindsay to sit at that desk in the front of the room, knowing that it belonged to a dead person. I wonder if he stored his gun in there. I wonder if she wonders the same thing.

124

"Mr. Messier, who do you think the true hero is, Kurtz or Marlow?"

I look up from the doodle I didn't even realize I was making on the corner of my notebook.

"Uh," I say. I turn a few pages of our book, *Heart of Darkness,* and try to remember who's who. "Uhhh," I say again.

She sighs. "Ms. Mead?"

Lacy Mead blushes and shrugs.

Ms. Lindsay looks like she's going to cry. She searches the room for someone more reliable.

"Ms. Lear? How about you?"

Grace Lear, of course, has a lengthy opinion delivered in a way that does not invite anyone to disagree with her. She probably signed up for this class for fun. I tune her out and stare at the empty desk in front of me.

It belongs to Claire Harris.

Damn.

Claire.

I've had a crush on her since second grade when we were paired together on the school field trip to the Science Museum. We had to hold hands from when we got off the bus until we reached the front steps of the museum. Those were the best four minutes of my life.

OK, so I'm exaggerating. They probably weren't the

best four. But they were pretty great, all things considered. She was in the grade above me, so already she had an air of mystery. She had long hair back then, and she wore it parted on the side, with a little blue barrette that she constantly unclasped, then smoothed her hair across her forehead, and clasped the barrette again. She did this all the way to the museum. She was so cute. Still is. The teacher paired us up and told us we had to hold hands with our "buddy" until we got to the steps of the museum. When the chaperone paired me with Claire, I felt the way I imagined it would feel to win the lottery.

When she took my hand, hers was warm and soft and surprisingly strong. She wasn't afraid to hold on tight. She took her task as my buddy very seriously, as if I needed extra protection. I didn't mind. I remember not being sure if I should squeeze back or not. I concentrated on returning the squeeze in equal measure. I didn't want her to think I was a wimp, after all. We walked side by side, following Cal and Dylan. They didn't want to hold hands. They kept letting go when the chaperones weren't looking. But Claire was a rule follower, and I was happy to let her hold tight. Cal and Dylan kept turning back to make kissy faces at us. They were so jealous it was oozing out of them. I just smirked.

I'm not sure when our arms started swinging as we

walked, but it felt natural. And happy. Like this was something Claire and I did all the time. But when we got to the door and the teacher said we could let go, the magic disappeared. My hand was empty again. I tried to feel the ghost of hers in my palm, but I couldn't. All I felt was the cold emptiness she'd left there. She skipped off with her best friend, Grace, without turning back, and I didn't see her again until the end of the day, when once again we held hands, arms swinging, all the way back to the bus.

As soon as we were all settled in our seats, she fixed her hair again. She was sitting in front of me, and I watched how she carefully finger-combed her hair to the side, then slid the barrette in place. I was close enough to hear the click of the clasp. She stared out the window, even as Grace chattered at her. It was as if she'd gone off someplace else. Like I do sometimes. Only right then, I'd wished we'd gone off together.

For a long time after that, I'd find myself staring out the window trying to imagine what she was dreaming about that day—and if it was ever the same thing as me.

Sometimes now, when I watch her around school, I'll catch her eye and she'll smile at me, and I think she sees the real me. It's probably wishful thinking. For all I know, she's just smiling at me out of pity. But sometimes when I see her hanging out with her friends, I think she looks like how I feel when I hang out with my friends; just a little apart. A loner, even though she isn't alone. Like she's looking for something but she's not sure what. Just like she did on the bus when we were seven years old. Just like I still do sometimes, when I'm hanging with Cal and Dylan. Sometimes when they're talking, it's like I've heard the same comments, the same stories, the same jokes and insults so many times, they've lost their meaning. Or maybe I have.

I just want to hear something new for once. Do something new. *Be* something new.

Sometimes I imagine risking everything and asking Claire out.

Hey, Claire, I'd say. *How's it goin'?*

Hey, Jack, she'd say, and smile and fix her hair the way she's been doing since she was seven.

Did you know I've had a crush on you for, like, eight years? I'd ask confidently.

She'd laugh and push me in a flirty way. And then I'd say, *So, will you go out with me?*

And in my dream, her eyes look into mine.

I thought you'd never ask, she'd say.

And then we'd both laugh and magically be the couple I always dreamed of. And Cal and Dylan would be jealous but not in a horrible way. And Claire would join us in the car and sit in the Look How Ugly You Are seat, only she wouldn't mind, because she's beautiful. She'd lean her head on my shoulder as we drove through town, and we'd know, as we looked out the window, that we were both dreaming about the same thing. Our life, together, someday, away from here.

The bell rings and we all get up in our typical herdlike way. Desk legs scrape as we try to disentangle ourselves. Backpack zippers thrum in unison. The line bottlenecks at the door. Ms. Lindsay goes back behind her desk and ruffles through papers. She gathers them together and taps the pile on her desk to straighten them. She seems a bit overly tidy.

"Stop being obvious," Dylan mumbles in my ear.

"Huh?"

He nudges his head in Ms. Lindsay's direction. "Checking her out."

"No, I wasn't."

"Why not? Everyone else does."

"Never mind."

I finally squeeze through the door and step into the slow and somewhat steady flow of people walking to their next class. Mine is gym with Cal and Dylan. We all tried to get out of it, but now that we don't play sports, no such luck. Cal's already in the locker room when Dylan and I got there.

"You two are late enough," he says.

Dylan drops his backpack on the floor. It sounds like a bag of cement hitting the ground.

"Jesus, D. What the hell do you have in there?" Cal asks.

He shrugs. "Just stuff."

Cal pushes it with his foot.

"Don't touch!" Dylan says.

Cal laughs it off, but I can tell he really does wonder, and now I do too.

We change and meander out to the gym. A bunch of people are already shooting hoops. Ms. Sawyer, the gym teacher, looks extra frazzled.

"I heard some freshman broke his finger in first period," Cal tells us. He smirks. "His middle one."

"Awesome," Dylan says.

We shoot some hoops until Ms. Sawyer breaks us up into teams, and as usual I end up wearing a stupid red pinny. It smells like a hundred different people's sweat. I don't think she ever washes the things. It makes me want to puke.

We spend the next thirty-five minutes halfheartedly dribbling the ball up and down the court. No one really seems to care who wins. Half the time, whoever has the ball dribbles around in circles and tries to show off, acting like a Harlem Globetrotter reject. Then Ms. Sawyer blows her whistle, and we all go back to the locker room to change. No one showers because no one dares to set foot in the shower stalls, which make the pinnies look like they just came from the dry cleaners.

I wonder if the girls' locker room is this scary.

Cal pushes his toe against Dylan's bag. "What the hell's in there, anyway?" he asks again. This time, he doesn't bother to wait for Dylan to answer or stop him. He bends down and grabs the bag.

"Hey! That's private!" Dylan lunges for it but misses.

Cal gets this weird look on his face, then reaches in and pulls out a gray brick. It looks like one of those pavers people use to line their gardens or driveways or whatever. "What the . . . ?"

"Why the hell do you have a brick in your bag?" I ask.

Dylan grabs it from Cal and puts it back inside. "None of your business."

I can think of only two reasons someone would have a brick in their bag:

A. To break a window.
B. To break someone's head.

Since Dylan is not a violent kid, I'm going with A. But why?

"Talk to us, D.," Cal says.

Dylan slumps down on the bench between us. "It's stupid," he says.

"True." I sit next to him. "There are no good reasons to carry a brick in your bag. Unless you plan to build a fort, which, well, is not much of a fort if you only have one."

"Who's the unlucky bastard you plan to use this on?" Cal asks.

"He's not using it on *anyone*," I say.

"I'm not going to *hurt* anyone," Dylan says. "I just . . . never mind. You wouldn't understand. "

I reach for the bag, but he grabs it away.

"Whoever it is isn't worth getting in trouble for," I say. "And you know that's exactly what will happen."

He stands up. "I'm doing this," he tells us. "And if you guys are my friends, you won't try to stop me."

We watch him, then look at each other for some wordless agreement about whether to tackle him for the bag. But before we can get our telepathic communication at the right frequency, Dylan bolts and is out the door with a lead on us that means we will never catch him.

"Wow," Cal says. "That was weird."

"What are we gonna do?" I ask.

He shrugs. "A guy's gotta do what a guy's gotta do, I guess."

"Shouldn't we try to stop him?" I can't believe Cal's so nonchalant.

"I say we follow him from a distance and see what he's up to. If it looks bad, we'll step in." He nods, like this is a brilliant plan.

He seems a little too hungry for some excitement, all of a sudden.

Why am I the only one who sees this for what it is: insane?

We rush out to the hall to see which way Dylan went. It's the end of the day, so the halls are a madhouse, with people shoving their way out of our group holding cell. Luckily Dylan is tall, and we can see his mop of shaggy brown hair bobbing between the traffic up ahead. We shove our way through as best we can, keeping enough distance so he doesn't realize we're following him. Normally after school we meet up in the parking lot at Cal's car, but today Dylan goes out the exit where the bus pickup is. I turn to see what Cal wants to do. He motions for me to keep going.

Just as I think we are being totally covert spies, Dylan is standing in front of us. "Fine. If you're just going to follow me anyway, let's take the Great White."

Cal nods and we go back to the other parking lot and climb in.

III.

The car has been sitting in the sunny lot with the windows rolled up, so it's hot inside and stinks to high heaven. As soon as Cal starts the engine, we all roll down our windows and hang our heads out.

"Told you it wasn't my feet," says Dylan.

"Well, they don't help, that's for sure," I say.

"Where to?" Cal asks.

Dylan sticks his head out the window and takes a deep breath. "No questions. Just go."

"Why?"

"No questions. Just go."

Cal shrugs and pulls out of the parking spot. We drive through the lot with the music blasting, as usual. *Boom bah-bah, BOOM bah-bah.*

I lean forward to see Dylan's reflection in the side mirror. He seems to have a far too serious and determined expression on his face to be up to anything good.

As always, the school parking lot is packed and completely bottlenecked at the one and only exit. It's a really good thing that our school has never had one of those crazy shooting sprees because no one would be able to escape. The car idles. The cool November breeze mixes with the usual school smells of stale cologne, cafeteria, and car exhaust, and drifts through the car.

"Dylan!" a girl yells. Sammy, his sister, runs toward us. She's wearing her cheerleading uniform and looking extraordinarily hot, as usual. What is *un*usual is the fact that she is not only acknowledging Dylan's existence but using his name and coming toward us. The outcasts. Sammy sits at the jock table surrounded by basketball players and cheerleaders. She does not acknowledge our existence. Ever.

She runs over to Dylan's side of the car and leans her head in. Her perfume mixes with the ugly and banishes it.

"Hey," she says. "Can you tell Mom I don't need a ride home tonight? The battery on my phone died. We have an away game, so I won't be home till late."

"How are you getting home?" Dylan asks.

She sighs. "Jacob."

"Gross."

"He's not gross."

Cal coughs and says "asshole" at the same time.

Cal's crush on Sammy is kind of like my crush on Claire. Hopeless. Sammy will never be in our arena. She is a Popular Girl for the Popular Crowd. Not for us outliers. Sammy is destined to always be under the arm of the captain of something sporty. Not the chess club. (Not that any of us are in the chess club. But we're a lot closer to that than any sort of sport.)

"Subtle, Cal," Sammy says.

"You know my name?" Cal pats his chest where his heart should be.

"Can you just let her know?" Sammy asks.

"Yeah. Be good. OK?" Dylan sounds so serious. And sad. His fingers clutch his backpack more tightly.

"I'm always good," Sammy says. "Maybe you should take your own advice." She winks at him and fluffs his hair. I've never seen them be so . . . brother-and-sister-ish. They're so good at pretending the other doesn't exist at school. But I know their secret, so I get why they would be close. They have to help each other keep their friends from finding out how they live. Stuff like that bonds you.

I bet Sammy would be horrified if she found out I knew about them. It's not really something Dylan and I

136

talk about at all. He's made it clear he doesn't want to. But I *do* know. And I guess that makes us closer than I am to Cal. Also, Dylan's just a lot nicer.

Until I met Dylan, I never knew there were people who lived with so much . . . stuff everywhere. Dylan says their mom can't help it. That must be true, because there's no way anyone could *want* to live like that. In complete chaos. My parents are neat freaks so the one time I stepped into Dylan's house, I was in shock. I had no idea Dylan lived that way, with boxes of clothes and magazines and newspapers stacked in strange heaps all over the place, even in the hall. When I see Sammy and Dylan at school, looking so normal, I forget what they go home to, and what that must be like. Looking at Sammy with her supermodel smile, her perfect hair, and her crisp-looking uniform, it's as if that other life doesn't exist. Somehow, she keeps herself separate from it.

We all watch her jog off, cheerleader skirt swinging.

"If either of you are looking at her butt, you're dead," Dylan says.

We keep watching.

"So, what's up with your sister and that douchebag Jacob?" Cal asks.

Dylan shrugs. "Who knows. I guess they might be dating. But it's not serious."

"You mean they haven't screwed yet," Cal says.

"Don't even go there."

"Well, that won't last long," Cal says. "Jacob isn't going to waste his time on someone who doesn't put out. Sorry, D., but it's the truth."

"Sammy doesn't put out," Dylan says. "For anyone." He's still clutching the brick.

"That's good news for you, Cal," I say.

"Like she'd ever look at me."

"Can we stop talking about my sister like she's a piece of meat, please?"

"I would never talk about her like that!" Cal says.

"Whatever." Dylan looks out the window, and we continue to inch forward in the parking lot.

I keep thinking about the brick in his backpack and wondering what Dylan has planned, who he could be so mad at, and why none of us knows about it. Maybe it has something to do with his mom. Or Sammy. My own sisters would kill me if I tried to defend their honor or anything like that. They kind of hate me, I think. Other than ditching the tandem mountain bike, my sisters are total do-gooders, like my parents. They started a Go Green campaign at their middle school. They stand by the trash at lunch and make sure people recycle properly.

They even collect food for compost and wheel the bin two blocks away to the community garden my parents helped start.

I do none of these things. I don't know if it's because I'm lazy or because I know I'll never be as perfect as the rest of them so why bother.

One time I caught my sisters trying to break into the clubhouse. They told me they'd smelled marijuana and "were concerned for my health and safety." They told me they were going to tell our parents if I didn't confess everything to them, and even then they would still tell if they thought I needed help. They're so naive, they didn't realize that I could just lie. Which I did. I said we tried smoking a little but it made us sick and we would never do it again.

They believed me.

The truth is, I didn't get sick. I got high. And I liked it. We all did. I guess lucky for us, pot is kind of hard to score if you don't know any potheads or have any other friends outside our circle of three. Or much money, for that matter.

"So, J.," Cal says. "What about you?"

I have no idea what he's asking.

"Huh?"

"D. has a thing for Ms. Lindsay—"

"No. I don't!" Dylan interrupts.

"Right. What was she wearing today? Something sexy?"

Dylan's face is bright red. "I don't remember," he lies.

Cal laughs. "OK. You both know I lust over Grace Lear."

"And Sammy," I point out.

"Not going there," Dylan says.

"What about you, Jack?" Cal asks.

If I don't answer, they'll harass me and accuse me of being on the other team. But if I tell the truth, they'll most likely do something to embarrass me in the most horrifying way possible.

"You don't know her," I lie. We're all pretty good at this. I don't know why I don't want them to know about Claire, but my feelings for her feel private. Like a secret wish that wouldn't come true if anyone else knew it.

"Um, the school's not *that* big," Cal says. "I'm pretty sure we know her."

"I don't know her name," I lie again.

"Right," Cal says. "C'mon, spill. We all did."

"Make someone up," I say. "Like you did for D."

Cal laughs. "Ms. Sawyer."

"That's the best you've got?" I ask. "Fine. I am madly

in love with Ms. Sawyer. Every night, I dream about her gym uniform and that whistle around her neck."

"No uniform," Cal jokes. "A pinny! With nothing under it!"

Dylan makes a gagging noise. "Oh my God. I will never be able to get that image out of my head. Thanks a lot!"

"Pinny and a whistle." Cal purses his lips and makes a loud whistle. "Oh, Jack. Jack, come here and score a three-pointer," he says in a high-pitched voice.

"What does that even mean?" I ask.

"I don't know—it just sounded good!"

"There has to be a basketball term that's at least a little more sexy," Dylan says.

"'Balls'?" I ask.

"How is 'balls' sexy?" Cal says. "It's a dude body part."

"Well, maybe she could say, 'I want to dribble your balls'?" Dylan suggests.

"What does *that* mean?" Cal asks.

Dylan shrugs. He still seems distracted.

"Ooh-ooh! Layup!" Cal says.

"How is that sexy?" I ask.

"You know. *Lay!*"

"Use it in a sentence," I say.

Cal taps his fingers on the dashboard. "Crap. You're right. Basketball just isn't sexy. Except for the pinnies. On a girl. With no bra."

"As long as she's not Ms. Sawyer," I add.

"I think she plays on the other team, anyway," Cal says.

"Why, just because she's a gym teacher?" I ask. "Nice stereotyping."

Cal shrugs. "I bet she hooks up with that computer teacher, Ms. Yung."

"Nah, she's hot for Ms. Lindsay like everyone else," Dylan says.

"Maybe all three of them get together," I say. "And Ms. Sawyer makes them wear pinnies."

We all laugh. It feels good. I look out the window and imagine Claire here beside me again. Not part of *this* conversation, obviously. But here, laughing with us. With me. I wonder where she is right now. I wonder if she's looking out a window like I am, and what she's thinking about. I wonder if she's ever thought of me or remembers that time we held hands. But I know it's probably hopeless. So I try to focus on the now. On here. On my friends.

Cal turns up the music so the bass thumps through my chest like an out-of-rhythm heartbeat. It makes me feel alive in a way I haven't for a while.

142

Maybe it's OK, after all, me just hanging with Cal and Dylan. Maybe this is good enough. Maybe, for now, there *isn't* more to life. Maybe there doesn't need to be.

But then I glance over at Dylan, who is still clutching his backpack, and I have a horrible feeling that what feels like "good enough" for now is about to change. That something is brewing, and maybe we are all going to have to decide who we want to be after all.

Dylan sees me staring at the backpack and gets all serious. "I hate this stupid parking lot," he says as we inch forward one more car length.

Normally, I do too. But right now, for the first time, I'm grateful to be stuck here. Stuck in the Great White with my best friends, no matter how screwed up they are.

It's hard to believe these same people earlier conned a poor guy out of forty bucks and gave him the finger for his trouble. How do we get from that to this? How do we lose ourselves like that and still somehow manage to find our way back to caring?

As I sit here and laugh about sexual basketball references, my best friend holds a weapon in his backpack. A weapon he may be afraid to use but plans to anyway.

These are the thoughts I have, staring out my window.

Not *There must be more to life* but *Please don't let there be*. That anything beyond this moment, any meaning our lives might have outside this car, scares me.

But we keep moving forward anyway.

Inch by inch.

FIVE:
DEATH OF A SALESMAN
(Stephen: 2:18 p.m.)

I.

BEN'S BREATH IS WET IN MY EAR. A WHISPER. "I'm sorry."

"Don't," I whisper back. "I can't do this anymore."

He squeezes my arm and presses his chest tighter against mine. We're hiding under the stairs at school. It smells dusty and full of secrets. Every time we hear footsteps above us, we pull apart, wait, then come together again. Every time, it hurts more.

We have the most impossible relationship in the world.

When we move away from each other for the third time, his eyes are glassy. He better not cry. I will kick his ass if he cries.

"I'm the one who should be crying," I say.

He wipes his eyes with the back of his hands.

"I'm sorry," he says again.

"I know that. All right? It doesn't actually solve anything, though."

"Why can't we just keep things like they are?"

"Because I don't like hiding under stairwells after school just to see you? I don't like lying to my friends? I don't like feeling that what we're doing is wrong?"

"You know it's harder for me," he says. "With basketball. My parents. My friends. I can't be open the way you are."

"You think I'm open? Hardly."

"You told Lacy."

"She's my best friend. Or was."

"She'll get over it."

"I doubt that. She's good friends with Grace. You're supposed to be dating Grace. You cheated on Grace with me. She has a fairly good reason to hate both of us."

"She's always hated me."

"Only the way sisters do. She only hates your lies."

He bangs the back of his head against the grimy wall. "What choice do I have? Do you know what my coach would do if he found out? He'd probably kick me off the team."

"Right. You know he can't do that."

"He'd find an excuse. Plus, hello? The team would kick the crap out of me."

"You don't know that."

He leans his head against the cinder-block wall and closes his eyes. "I know those guys, OK? There is no way they'd be cool if they found out I was—"

"Was what?"

"You know."

"Yeah. I know. I just don't know why you can't say it."

He reaches for my hand awkwardly. "Why do I have to say it? Why does this have to have a name?"

"Because it does have a name," I say. "If you really cared about me—about *yourself*—you would tell them. At the very least you would break up with Grace. She *saw* us, for God's sake. What, is Miss Perfect going to pretend she misunderstood what we were doing? How did you explain it to her, anyway?"

"I told her I was confused. That it wouldn't happen again."

I shake my head and start to leave. "Then, I guess it won't."

"Wait!" he says, reaching for me. "You make everything sound so easy. Like there was some switch someone clicked, and I'm this new person now—"

"I know it's not easy. But accepting who you are is . . . *necessary*."

He steps back. "I'm sorry," he says for the third time. Each time, it feels less true and more like an excuse.

"Me too," I say. "I have to go."

He grabs my arm again as I try to leave and pulls me to him. We kiss. Hard. Ninety-nine percent of me wants to stay. Right here. Forever. But the one percent pulls me off him.

"I can't do this anymore," I say. I step out from our hiding place under the stairs. School just got out and I know if I walk down the hall, he won't risk following me. Won't risk being seen with me. It hurts, but I wait a few seconds anyway. Just in case.

He stays under the darkened stairs, though, just like I knew he would.

The parking lot is in its usual chaotic state. I zigzag between parked cars until I find my mom's old Civic. Normally I have to take the bus, but she let me borrow it today because she wanted to walk to work. Inside, the car is toasty warm from being in the sun all day. I toss my bag on the backseat and lean back before starting the engine.

148

I don't want to go home.

I don't want to go anywhere.

I wish I could call Lacy. That's what I would have done before. But everything's different now that she left me for her cheerleader friends and I ruined her life by secretly seeing her brother.

"You're going to ruin everything for everyone," is what she said.

"Those girls are just using you to get to Ben," is what I said.

"You're wrong."

"You'll see."

We're still waiting.

Ben is still fake-dating Grace, but it's only a matter of time before someone figures stuff out. As soon as that happens, I'm sure Lacy's so-called new friends will dump her. People like Grace don't seek out people like me and Lacy to be friends with unless they want something. I'm just still shocked that Lacy (a) fell for it and (b) dumped me for them.

I jump when the passenger door opens.

"Hey," Ben says, and hops in the car, as if it's something he does every day.

Instinctively, I look around to see if anyone noticed.

"What are you doing?" I ask.

"I don't know," he says. "Let's just get out of here."

The traffic at school is terrible, though, and the longer we inch out of the parking lot, the more nervous I get.

My palms sweat around the steering wheel. I can feel the slippery wet between my fingers, but every time I move my hands, it makes a gross sticky noise, so I keep them where they are. I'm a nervous sweater. It kind of sucks.

We don't talk. Every time I glance over, I can see Ben's jaw twitching. He has a baseball hat on and is hunched low in the seat.

"Don't you have a basketball game tonight?" I ask.

"Yeah. So?"

I shrug. "Just figured you'd be with the team doing . . . whatever you do."

"Away game. The bus doesn't leave for a while. We have time."

"For?"

"I don't know."

When we finally pull out of the parking lot, he sits up a little. I wipe my hands on my jeans one at a time. I've only had my license for a few months, and I'm trying to keep my hands at the right points on the steering wheel. Trying to look in my rearview mirror, side-view mirror, and on the road in front of me all at the same time. Meanwhile, I can feel Ben's eyes on me.

"Sooooo," I finally say. "Where are we going?"

"Wherever. I just needed to see you. I didn't want to leave things like we did under the stairs."

"But . . . they're ending."

He looks out the window. "Yeah. I guess."

We drive for a while longer, until I decide I'll take him home. What's the point of dragging this out? When he realizes we're headed in that direction, he reaches over and awkwardly puts his hand on my thigh.

"I'm just really confused," he says.

"God. Please don't say that with your hand on my thigh. Seriously."

He takes his hand back.

"Those are your parents' words," I say. "Not yours. You *know* what you want. You're scared. That's not the same as confused."

From what I've gathered, there are two general reactions parents have when you come out to them: "supportive" and "not supportive."

"Supportive" first reactions: *Are you sure? Maybe you're just confused. It's natural to experiment. You're too young to know for sure. We love you no matter what, but . . . are you sure??*

"Not supportive" first reactions: *Over my dead body! You disgust me! You're going to hell! You're no longer my son/daughter! Get out of this house!*

My parents' first reaction: *We're so glad you told us. We're so glad you trust us. We're so proud of you, no matter what.* It could have been worse, but it was the *no matter what* that killed me. What does that mean? No matter how disgusting I am? That, and the brief look of disappointment I saw on my dad's face before he could hide it—the realization that, in addition to all his other failures, he failed to have a "normal" kid.

"My parents don't even know," Ben says.

"But that's what you think they'll say. That you're confused."

"What I think they'll say is nothing. Because they'll never know."

"Never? So . . . you're just going to hide who you are all your life? Your parents aren't complete jerks. They might be upset at first, but they'll get over it."

"You obviously don't know my parents."

"Lacy will support you."

"Lacy won't even *talk* to me."

"That's not because you're *gay*. God. She's mad because you're cheating on her new best friend with her old best friend."

He ignores that. "Listen. I just can't tell my parents. OK? I can't."

"Won't."

We're quiet again. I hate this. I hate him. I hate him because he's a jock. And he has a fake girlfriend. And he wants to go to college and keep being a jock and having fake girlfriends. I hate him because he is never going to change. Not even for me. It figures that out of all the gay guys at school (and let's face it, there aren't that many, but still) I have to fall for the dude with the fake girlfriend.

I pull up to the curb of his house. I wonder if Lacy's inside.

"I guess this is it, then," I say.

"It doesn't have to be."

I sigh. "It kind of does."

"Please, Stephen. Don't make me choose."

I look at him. I mean really look. At the guy who invited me to his house to watch movies but said I couldn't tell anyone. Who gave me my first boy kiss. First in his living room with the lights out, then in the stairwell at school. Who told me he had a girlfriend to keep his friends from finding out the truth. Who said sometimes she didn't feel like a lie. Who said sometimes he thinks he loves her. Who whispered her name, *Grace,* as if she was the secret instead of me. Who told me he really *was*

153

confused. So confused. Who cried, so I held him. Who, on a whim, kissed my neck between the stacks at the school library. Who punched me in the side when he realized someone saw. And cried again when he realized that someone was Grace.

Why does it have to be like this?

"I'm sorry," I say. "But you have to."

He opens the door but doesn't get out. Just waits. I'm not sure for what. I know neither of us wants it to end this way. But we also both know there's no point in staying together, either. If he has to make a choice, it won't be me.

He gets out. Before he shuts the door, he leans back in. His face is wet with tears again.

"I'm the one who's sorry," he says, and pushes the door shut.

II.

When I get home, my mom's standing in the driveway, waving excitedly.

"Where have you been? I've been waiting!" She runs over to the car.

"Did I miss something?" I ask.

"Your dad called. He said he has some news for us!"

"What is it?"

"You know your dad. He wants to surprise us."

She runs around to the other side of the car and gets in. "C'mon. Let's go meet him."

She's beaming—until she sees my face.

"What's wrong? You look terrible."

"It's nothing," I say. Because now that's true.

My mom reaches for my thigh and squeezes it exactly where Ben was touching me earlier. I push her hand away. "I said it's nothing."

She takes her hand back. "Whatever you say," she says sarcastically.

"So, why are we meeting Dad?" I ask to change the subject. "Is this about another 'job opportunity'?"

"Oh, honey, don't spoil it."

"I was just asking."

She doesn't answer. Now we're both in a bad mood. At least temporarily. My mom's bad moods last approximately thirty seconds.

The truth is, my dad has a lot of "job opportunities." Unfortunately, they all end in disappointment. This never seems to get my parents down, though. "Close, but no cigar," my dad always says. And my mom chimes in,

155

"Just wasn't meant to be. But that's OK! Something even better is right around the corner!"

It's hard living with eternal optimists. No matter how many times life craps on them, they wipe it off their faces and smile.

I seem to be the only one who has accepted the truth: there is nothing around that corner but more crap.

"Your father is really excited about this one, hon. He thinks this is it. The one. Finally!"

I turn for a brief second to give her my *Really?* look. As in *Really? You really believe this?* But the expression on her face, the hope, keeps me from following through. Instead, I say, "That's great. I hope he's right."

My eyes move from the speedometer to the road to the rearview mirror, in that order, for the next several minutes. Beside me, I can almost see the dream scene playing out in my mom's head. She believes it all so strongly, even though "it all" has never happened. We have never even come close to "it all." Not once. And honestly, after the day I've had? The last thing I need is to go hear my dad talk about what a great job opportunity he's found, when in reality it will probably go to someone else. Someone more pushy. More needy. More assertive. More . . . qualified.

My dad's best quality is the very thing that condemns him to a life of disappointment: he's too nice.

He will never be first because he is always holding the door open for someone else to go ahead of him. He's the poster guy for the saying "Nice guys finish last."

It's also why I love him.

I hate him and I love him. It hurts to see someone you love get hurt over and over. It also depresses the hell out of me. Why do I always end up with people I love and hate at the same time?

In ninth grade we had to read *Death of a Salesman,* and I was down and out for weeks. All I could think was, *My dad is Willy Loman.* He talks and talks about all these amazing things he's going to do and how successful he's going to be and how we're going to have this great house and new car and live in a nice neighborhood and go out for dinner and finally buy clothes from a real store instead of the thrift store in the city, where I pray every time I enter that no one I know will see me.

But my dad will never be rich. He will never get a job that lasts. He will never get respect. He will never be really happy even though he acts like happiness is nearly in sight. He will never be the someone he pretends to believe in when he looks in the mirror and forces himself to smile. More dead than alive. Willy Loman's biggest fear.

It's hard to know that about your dad. It must be even harder to know it about your husband. I can see the disappointment that has drawn itself across my mother's face in the deep worry lines that only get deeper. The mask of truth.

She doesn't reveal an ounce of doubt to my dad, though. She just cheers and consoles, cheers and consoles.

It makes me love and hate her, too.

"Take the interstate," she says as we approach the on-ramp.

I put my signal on and begin to merge onto the highway when a car blasts its horn at me. It must have been in my blind spot. The driver pulls up beside us in the other lane and gives us the finger. It's a guy driving a Volvo station wagon with two little kids in the backseat.

I wave at him, like *Yeah, yeah, sorry, my bad,* and he drives on.

"Did that man just give you the finger?" my mom asks. "He has two young kids in the car."

"I must have cut him off by accident."

"No, you didn't. He should have pulled over to let you in! If anyone deserves to get the finger, it's him." She whispers the last bit as if she can't bring herself to be nasty too loudly.

I burst out laughing. Partly because I'm so nervous and partly because it's hysterical. It feels strange to laugh, and I realize how pathetic that is. It's been too long.

"It's not funny!" my mom yells. She clutches the handgrip above her for dear life.

"It's OK, Mom," I say.

But she's all flustered. "I hate the finger. I hate it. Why do people do that? It's terrible."

"It's just a finger," I point out.

"But you didn't deserve it. His poor children had to see that, too. Ugh."

"Mom, don't get hysterical. It's no big deal." I reach over and touch her arm reassuringly. "Really."

"Both hands on the wheel," she says. But she lets go of the bar with her other hand and touches her arm where I touched it and smiles.

"We're going to Little Cindy's, by the way," she says. "Exit six."

"Little Cindy's? Really?"

"It's our place. You know that."

Of course it is. We're talking about my mom and dad, after all. Their place couldn't be a cool café somewhere.

Or a nice upscale restaurant. No. It has to be a crappy chain restaurant whose sign is of a little girl with pigtails. *This* is my parents' romantic meet-up. I'm telling you.

"I wish you wouldn't make fun," my mom says. "You know the story. You know why it's special."

"Yeah, I know."

When my parents were in high school, my dad was a cashier there. My mom and her friends would go and give him a hard time. My poor dad would have to wait on them and ask all the usual required questions about what flavor milk shake they wanted, and they'd make these crazy orders to hold the onions and add extra tomatoes and all kinds of stuff just to torture him. One day an argument broke out between a customer and another cashier. This is my mom's favorite part of the story, and every time she tells it my dad gets a little more heroic. My dad leaped over the counter to fight the guy, but before anything happened, the supervisor came out and fired my dad on the spot, even though the cashier and all the other customers said my dad was just defending her. My mom says the moment he jumped the counter was the moment she fell in love with him.

I don't think my dad has done anything heroic since, but it doesn't matter. At that moment, my mom saw his potential. His *goodness,* she says.

So that's why Little Cindy's. It's where their lives together began. And, according to my mother, a reminder to my dad of what he's capable of.

"I've never told you this," my mom says. "But that place is special to me for another reason, too."

"What's that?"

"It reminds me of a time I stopped being so shallow and learned to look at people for who they really are, not what they seem. I was changed that day, as much as your dad."

I still have trouble imagining my dad in this scenario they've played out for me a million times over the years. It's hard to imagine my dad as the strong guy, the hero, that all kids want their dads to be. Because one question overshadows it all: What the heck happened to him?

And by mistake, I ask it out loud.

"What do you mean, 'What happened'?"

I grip the steering wheel more tightly. "Never mind," I say.

She looks out the window, ashamed of me. I deserve it.

But I do want to know. What happened to the handsome, muscular, brave man in the Little Cindy's uniform? When did he become the slouching, potbelly guy with the receding hairline? When did he start wearing his sad-dad uniform?

When did he stop being a hero?

This time, I am sensitive enough not to ask out loud.

We inch through traffic. My mom rolls down the window a crack, even though the breeze from outside is November cold.

"People grow up," she says. "People have to make sacrifices. For their family. Your dad, he always wanted to go to law school. Or be a real-estate agent. Or maybe a banker. Or something that required him to wear a suit. You know. A businessman. But . . ."

She looks over at me guiltily. I burned her, now it's my turn to get a sting. I kind of want it, at this point.

"When I got pregnant, things had to be put on hold for a while. Your dad didn't want you being raised by strangers in a day-care center, so I quit school and stayed home, and he . . ."

Oh, crap. Never mind. I don't want the sting after all. Please don't say it.

"He quit school to work full-time. Things were tight."

So who my dad became was . . . my fault? Am I the reason the hero she fell in love with turned into . . . Dad?

"That's why Dad never got his dream," I say.

I sense her shaking her head. "Well, he's getting it today."

162

III.

We pull into the Little Cindy's parking lot. It seems kind of crowded for late afternoon, since it's not really dinnertime yet. Lots of people from school come here because it's cheap and a place to go instead of home. But I hate it here. The minute you step inside, all you can smell is this nasty fried meat smell—and I'm not talking about the kind of smell that makes your mouth water. I'm talking about the kind of greasy dead animal smell that makes you gag. I came a few times at the beginning of the year, but couldn't stand smelling like a dead chicken when I left. I don't know what the appeal is. I guess it's a step above McDonald's or something. Anyway, people show up. Grab tables. Give the poor people who work here a hard time, laughing together because goofing on some poor schmuck behind the counter is apparently the funniest thing in the world. Sit around. Tell everyone what they just did because they have nothing better to talk about, even though everyone saw them do it. Repeat. It's not really my idea of a good time.

I find an open spot in the parking lot and practice my mad three-point parking skills. My mother sucks in her breath as I make the last turn and slide into the space. I don't blame her for being nervous. It's not as if I've had a lot of practice yet. But I manage to get the car between the white lines.

I cut the engine and wipe my sweaty hands on my jeans. We spot my dad's empty Ford Taurus across the way and head inside. I walk slowly, letting my mom go ahead of me a bit. I realize that I might know some people here from school, and they are about to see me with my parents, and possibly my parents behaving very emotionally. This all has the potential to be the most embarrassing moment of my life. An image of my dad jumping up from some ketchup-stained table and running across the restaurant toward us, arms outstretched, picking my mom up and swinging her around in a circle, flashes in front of me.

Please no.

My mom pauses at the door like I'm supposed to open it for her. I mean I know I am, but, just this once, couldn't she pretend not to know me? For pity's sake?

I take a deep breath and open the door. A flood of warm, greasy chicken air engulfs us. My mom cranes her neck around like a turkey to spot my dad. Most of the tables are taken by kids from school or old people. There's a long line at the counter that snakes through a maze marked by a metal railing. A few girls are sitting on the top rung, laughing and snapping their gum.

"There he is!" my mom says way too loudly. She grabs my hand as if I'm five and starts to drag me across the restaurant. I twist free (kind of like a five-year-old) and pray to God no one saw. My mom winds her way through the tables, stepping over backpacks left on the floor. My dad's sitting at a big table all by himself, and most likely being silently cursed by everyone in the room for taking a huge table for himself.

He stands up and opens his arms to us. Only my mom walks into them. He hugs her tight, just like I envisioned. Thankfully, he does not swing her around. We all take our seats. Me across from them.

"Well?" my mom says. "Are you going to keep us in suspense?"

He beams at me. I'm not proud, but the first thing that pops into my head is, *What Willy Loman story are you going to try to sell us this time?*

I feel terrible.

"Wait," he says. He takes a deep breath. "I want to savor this moment."

"Walt," my mom says, giggling. "You're such a goof."

They're holding hands on top of the table. I scan the

room for people I know. I recognize a bunch from school but don't see anyone I actually know-know, thank God. Not that there are many that would fall in that category.

"As you are aware," he says, all serious, "I had a job interview today."

"We know!" my mom says. "Now tell us what happened!"

"First, the interview lasted nearly three hours," my dad says matter-of-factly. His face is glistening with sweat. He's wearing his old brown suit, and I notice the elbow area is threadbare. It makes me sad. My dad has horrific taste in clothes. He wears light-blue polyester-type shirts with a breast pocket and brown pants and jacket of a similar material. This is his uniform. I'm surprised that these clothes are actually for sale anywhere. In fact, they probably aren't. My dad has been wearing them forever. Probably since before I was even born. If it weren't for the thinning hair and the fact that he's old, his clothes might even pass for retro cool. But they don't. Because my dad is wearing them.

"Three hours!" my mom says. "You must be exhausted."

"It was intense, that's for sure." He grins.

"What's the job, Dad?" I ask, trying to sound as enthusiastic as possible.

"Managorial," he says. He reaches below the table and fiddles in his pants pocket with his free hand, then pulls out a yellowed handkerchief. I'm pretty sure I am the only person under the age of fifty who has a parent who still uses a handkerchief. He carefully dabs the sweat off his face with it.

"Sorry," he says. "I'm still nervous! Can't seem to calm down."

My mom uses her free hand to pat him on the shoulder. "Well, you'd better tell us the news before we all need that thing," she says.

I could be sweating buckets and I would not touch that handkerchief.

"OK, OK," he says. He sits up taller. "They made an offer."

My mom screams. Everyone looks over at us. She claps her hand over her mouth, then hugs my dad.

When they finally pull apart, they are both crying.

I glance around the restaurant, horrified. But everyone has already gone back to eating. No one seems to care that my parents just hugged and kissed in public. No one cares that they are sobbing tears of joy.

If that was Ben and me, everyone would be staring. Let's face it. Two guys kissing is still a rarity. The captain of the basketball team kissing *me* in public would be epic.

167

I touch my bruised mouth and think of the two of us, hiding in the stairwell. Of Ben's tears.

My parents don't realize how lucky they are. They don't realize how easy they have it, being able to love each other in public like that. Ben and I could be as out as flags on the Fourth of July, and we still wouldn't get that kind of pass. Everyone would stare. Everyone would snicker. Everyone would judge.

It's hard to believe I could ever feel jealous of my parents, but right now I kind of do.

"We're so proud of you, honey," my mom says, wiping my dad's face. "We have to celebrate! Stephen, why don't you get in line for some milk shakes. Chocolate, right, honey?"

"Sure, sure. That would be great," my dad says. "And French fries. Remember how we used to dip 'em in our shakes?"

My mom smiles at him. "Of course I do." She lets go of his hand and fumbles in her purse for some money.

"What flavor do you want, Mom?" I ask.

"Chocolate. Of course!"

They beam up at me, faces still glistening. So happy. Despite what happened with Ben earlier, I admit I feel happy too. My dad's dream actually came true. Damn. He finally did it!

I take the money and go to the back of the line and wait. The group in front of me is definitely from my school but older. Maybe seniors. They're talking about the colleges they're applying to and how they hope to get as far away from here as possible. Good plan.

The chicken smell mixed with the person's cologne in front of me is making me feel nauseous.

Every few minutes, we move forward a couple of feet, then wait. Pretty soon three guys get in line behind me. I know two of them from my lit. elective, but we don't talk much. Jack Messier and Dylan something. They're in the grade below me, so we weren't friends when we were younger, and at my school, it seems the friend cliques that formed in elementary school stay that way, except in rare cases. Like Lacy and me, who became friends because we never belonged to a clique, and I guess eventually we circled around the outside long enough that we bumped into each other.

I touch my phone in my back pocket and think maybe I should call her. Try one more time. But I know it's hopeless. She was so hurt when I told her the girls were just using her to get closer to Ben. She didn't want to hear it. And then when she caught Ben and me together one night at her house, it sent her over the edge.

"*You're* the one using me! Not them!"

And just like that, we went from being best friends to strangers.

Jack nudges Dylan, and he kind of falls into me.

"Sorry," he says, not even looking at me.

He's carrying a backpack that he keeps rehiking over his shoulder. He also keeps glaring at one of the guys behind the counter who appears to be giving orders to everyone else. Dylan sort of looks like he wants to kill him. Then the friend I don't know grabs him and starts pulling him back. They all turn to peer out across the dining room at . . . my dad.

"Uh-oh, isn't that the guy from this morning?" one of them whispers.

My dad gets up. He's looking at them like he knows them.

"Crap. We need to get out of here," Jack says.

My dad is striding toward them, his hand raised up like he wants to get their attention. But they bolt, running out the door. My dad hurries to the glass door just as it swings closed. He stands there, watching them run across the parking lot and jump into their car and take off. He stands in front of the glass, watching them go. He shakes his fist at them. "I know what you did!" he yells. "I'll report you!" Then he gives them the finger. But they're gone.

170

He keeps standing there, though, tapping his middle finger against the glass. It's not like my dad. Not like him to make a scene. Not like him to give anyone the finger. I look over to see if my mom—the finger hater—sees him, but it's too crowded, and all I can see is the top of her head poking up, trying to see what's going on.

I get out of line and run over to my dad. Up close, he looks even more not right. Not himself. He looks . . . crazed.

"Dad?" I ask, "Are you OK?"

He's still staring out the window.

"That was those boys from this morning," he says.

"What do you mean?"

"Thugs. They scammed me." He says it so quietly. "They . . . pulled a fast one on me. I knew it. But what could I do? Those boys are bad. You stay away from them." His hand reaches up to his chest. "They targeted me, those boys. Somehow they knew . . ."

"Dad? What's wrong."

"My chest feels funny," he says. "I'm not sure—"

He clutches my arm with his other hand. So tight. I grab him, but he's sinking to the floor.

"Walt!" my mom screams. She pushes her way through the people who have stood up to see my dad and me. "Walt!" she screams again.

But he only stares up at us. No, not at us. At the ceiling.

"Oh my God, Walt! Someone call nine-one-one," my mom yells.

A bunch of people pull out their phones as my mom and I crouch down and try to loosen my dad's shirt and lift his head up. My mom pats his cheeks. "Walt? Walt?"

She's shaking.

A guy in a Little Cindy's uniform pushes through to us. It's the guy Dylan looked like he wanted to kill.

"What happened?" he asks, crouching next to my mom. His name tag says DEWEY HARTSON. Dewey. Now, that is one unfortunate name. I don't know why I have this thought when my dad is on the floor, maybe dying. It just stands out. Everything does. Feet surround us. Black Converse. Bright-red running shoes. Silver ballet flats. That's all I see. Colorful feet encircling my parents on the greasy floor.

"I think he's having a heart attack," my mom yells at Dewey's face.

"Are there any doctors here?" Dewey calls out.

No one answers.

"Walt!" my mom says again, lightly tapping my dad's face. His head is resting against her thighs now. She's kneeling at his head.

"Maybe you should splash water on his face," some-one suggests.

"Someone get some water!" Dewey yells.

A girl who looks like she might be a senior runs over with a cup of water. My mom holds it to my dad's lips and tips it up, but the liquid just dribbles down the side of his face.

My mom looks over at me. I reach for her arm. "Help's coming," I say. Which is probably the lamest thing I could possibly tell her, but what else is there?

Her eyes are filled with worry and fear.

I squeeze her arm. "He'll be OK," I say, pretending.

Dewey glances around desperately. "Did you call nine-one-one?" he asks no one in particular.

A boy holds up his phone. "They're on their way. They're asking a bunch of questions."

"Give me that thing!" Dewey says.

The boy hands his phone over.

"Yeah. This is the manager. We've got a customer on the floor." He studies my dad while the person on the other end asks him questions. It's like he's watching a hurt animal, not a person, the way he scrunches his face.

"I don't know. Maybe two minutes ago? Yeah. Yeah. No, he's not responding. Loosen his shirt more!" he says to my mom.

I help her unbutton it. My dad's not wearing a T-shirt underneath, and sweaty black hairs pop out as soon as they're set free. His belly is going up and down, which is a relief. But it seems to be doing so very slowly.

"Give him some room!" Dewey says. The shoes step back, leaving us like an island on the sticky tile floor.

"I hear sirens!" someone yells.

The crowd, oddly, cheers.

"Help's coming," my mom whispers in my dad's face. "Hang on, Walt. Just hang on."

Seconds later an ambulance pulls up outside the door, and three EMTs come running in. The crowd parts for them. One starts talking to my mom while the other two pull out instruments and things from their bags and slap them on my dad.

I stand up and step back, watching. Watching like this is a movie I fell inside of. But I can't hear anything. My ears are ringing. My body is tingling. I don't feel the floor under my feet. I just keep stepping backward until someone's hands are on my arms, squeezing, and a faint voice is saying, "Whoa, sit down. Here you go. Give this kid some air."

It's Dewey. He comes around and faces me when I sit and asks if I'm all right. He has huge arm muscles and his shirt, I realize now, is way too tight. For some reason I

174

think of my mom's description of my dad when he was a hero all those years ago. Is this what she saw? Something like this? Is this what my dad used to be?

Behind him, I watch the EMTs bring in a stretcher. They surround my dad and carefully lift him up onto it. My mom hovers nearby and follows them.

He was so close, I think. He had the dream in his hand. I should have known something would keep him from having it come true.

Willy Loman. Willy Loman, I hate you.

"I have to go," I say. I get up and nearly fall. I want to throw up. Dewey guides me outside and to the ambulance. My mom starts to get in after my dad, then turns and sees me, remembering I'm here.

"You can drive right behind us," one of the EMTs tells my mom.

She nods and hurries over to me.

"Are you sure you should drive?" Dewey asks her.

She looks at him, foggy. Confused. Maybe she sees my old hero dad, too, when she looks at him.

"Yes," she says quietly. "Yes. Come on, Stephen."

I follow her to the car. She gets in on the passenger side. I take a deep breath and try to get a hold of myself. Focus. Breathe.

He is not Willy Loman.

He is not.

You did not make this happen.

He is not Willy Loman.

"Stephen," my mom says. "Let's go."

Behind the wheel, things become more clear. Key. Ignition. Turn. Put in reverse. I pull out behind the ambulance, its siren blasting. The hospital is close by, thank God.

My mom is clutching the bar on the passenger side again. But this time, she is not tapping her fingers. This time, she is not willing me to slow down but to go faster.

"What was he doing?" she asks me. "I don't understand."

"I don't know," I say.

"He just got up and hurried to the door. Who was he yelling at?"

"I don't know," I say again. I don't know why I don't want to tell her about the boys.

Thugs, my dad said. Those guys did something to him. Something mean. Something bad enough to break his heart.

"Oh, Walt," my mom says to the windshield.

"He'll be OK," I say. And I pray, pray, pray that's true.

She shakes her head. "The world doesn't want him to

176

succeed," she says, crying. "Why doesn't the world want him to succeed?"

I don't know how to answer. But all I can think is *Willy Loman* again. I can't get him out of my head.

I see my dad standing at that window, and it seems he is not giving those guys the finger—he is giving it to the world. And right now, it feels like the world deserves it. The *world* broke his heart.

"He's going to be OK," I say again.

She reaches over and squeezes my thigh.

"He has to be," she says.

"He will," I tell her. I will not let him become another Willy Loman. I won't.

I press harder on the gas pedal, and we race after the ambulance.

"Careful," my mom says. "But hurry."

We continue on, determined to save my dad, once a hero.

My dad, who deserves a chance to show the world it hasn't won.

SIX:
THAT GIRL ON THE WALL
(Keith: 2:47 p.m.)

1.

THE FIRST TIME I SAW THAT GIRL ON THE wall, I knew she was bad news.

She stood there like she was on a stage of her own making.

The graffiti backdrop seemed just a little too perfect for the real world.

She twisted her cigarette prop expertly in her fingers. Not smoking it. I don't think it was even lit.

She was only bad news because she wanted to be.

She seemed to want anyone who dared to walk down her side of the street to be afraid. To feel like they didn't belong.

It worked.

She showed up after summer vacation. Maybe she'd been there all summer. I don't know.

I only use the street to walk home from school.

But now it's her place.

And all fall, she's been letting me know it.

Her friends are like backdrops, too. Standing not next to but behind her. Looking where she looks.

Disapproving of what she disapproves of.

They are her handpicked backup dancers, with costumes just like hers:

High-heeled boots and short-short skirts or cut-off
    shorts.
Black tights with holes at the knee or thigh.
Too-tight tank tops.
Bare arms crossed at their chests when they aren't
    twirling their own cigarette props.
Moving to the music coming from a window nearby.

When I walked down the street, she jerked her chin at me.

Let her eyes travel up and down my scrawny body.

Her mouth made a curled-up expression of disapproval.

Like I am not her kind. Don't belong on her street.

The girls behind her made catlike noises to echo her body language.

She was right.

I am not her kind.

But maybe not in the way she thinks.

I couldn't help watching her, though.

Because she was beautiful, even with the cigarette and the curled-up lip.

She stepped forward, twirling her cigarette.

Whatyoulookinat?

She said it loud and tough. Fast. Like the four words were one.

Whatyoulookinat.

Like a bully would say just before he punches you in the face.

Maybe she could sense, even on that first day, that I was looking at *her*.

The her she seemed meant to be.

This her.

Not the one at school.

There, she wears jeans and a hoodie that seems to swallow her.

Same as most of her actors.

They sit at a corner table in the caf at school.

Trying to be invisible like everyone else, besides the jocks and beauty queens.

There, she tries to hide. Blend in.

In the one class we're in together, she slides down low in her seat.

Wears her hood even though it's against the rules.

It's the only trace of her rebellious side.

This her doesn't belong in *that* place.

I wondered if she recognized me from that place, too.

Is that why she curled her lip? And dared me to walk on her own turf?

Whatyoulookinat.

Maybe.

I almost stopped walking but tripped instead. My face burned.

The bones in my legs had turned to flimsy cardboard that couldn't hold me up.

She smirked but didn't laugh out loud. Too cool to let the sound leave her lips.

I walked faster the closer I got, knowing I should look down at the pavement as I passed.

Or at the sky.

Or anywhere but toward her stage.

My eyes didn't care about *should,* though.

They crossed the narrow street to find her as I

struggled with my cardboard legs. Forcing them to move one foot in front of the other.

Her hair was long and black and patent-leather shiny.

Her cigarette dangled dangerously from her left hand.

I was wrong about the prop.

A tiny swirl of gray escaped from the tip, up and around her bare arm. Like a pet snake-ghost.

She was a smoking statue queen.

She sneered at me as I watched.

I still couldn't stop.

She took another step forward. Stuck out her chest, proud and unashamed. Daring me to look right there.

But it was her eyes I wanted to look at.

Her friends moved in closer.

Ooooh. You show him, girl.

Like she was about to come after me. And kick me off their street.

They weren't the same cast as the quiet group in the caf, hiding under their baggy sweatshirts and tight jeans.

Here, they were fearless.

I picked up my pace and tried to get past them without tripping again.

But the smooth, even pavement suddenly felt like waves under my feet.

They all laughed as I walked past with wobbly legs.

I don't know why I looked back once I'd made it beyond them.

Whatyoulookinat? she asked again.

My cheeks felt like a candy fireball after you lick the sweet part off.

I shrugged, willing the heat to melt away.

I stopped and stood there while she waited for an answer.

She jerked her head at me, then lifted her fist in my direction, like a threat.

Then, her skinny middle finger slowly rose out of her fist in a wordless gesture.

But I didn't feel the silent insult.

If she couldn't say it out loud, I couldn't hear it.

Wouldn't.

Maybe she didn't want me to.

She swiveled around on her heel so all I could see was her long black hair—a leather cape cascading down her back.

Or a curtain falling, letting me know the show was over.

I turned and fled.

II.

That night I dreamed about her and that skinny finger and her hair and her angry face.

And the sound of her voice.

Whatyoulookinat?

As if she had to ask.

At school, I searched for her. For the others, too.

But they were like silent shadows, moving through the crowd. Pretending not to see me.

Pretending I couldn't see them.

Like we were each other's secret.

I didn't tell anyone about them.

Not even my best friend, Nate.

I don't know why.

On my way home the next day, I paused at the same street and considered skipping a block just in case she was there again.

Even though I wanted to see her, I didn't want *her* to see my skinny cardboard legs.

Didn't want to be sneered at by her crew. *Hisssssss.*

But my feet wouldn't let me skip her street.

I wobbled forward and spotted her right away.

She was standing on her stage, laughing with her friends.

I wondered what was so funny. Because they hadn't seen me yet.

She leaned her long graceful back against her graffiti-covered wall like she was a part of it. Like it was holding her up.

Or maybe it was the other way around.

She took a deep slow drag from her cigarette and blew tiny clouds of gray into the sky.

I walked slowly so I could watch her a little before she knew I was there.

When her friends saw me, they got all excited and walked to the edge of their stage.

Oooh, Sapphie. Here comes your boyfriend.

Sapphie. Sapphire.

The blue gemstone.

Hard, cold, beautiful . . . and precious.

She cleared her throat real loud and stood with one hand on her hip, the other holding that miniature baton cigarette.

Her actors moved closer to the edge of their stage, ready to attack.

She looked me up and down without shame.

Like I was something she might like to hunt. To taste.

And maybe spit out.

I waited for her to make up her mind.

She jerked her chin at me.

Whatyoulookinat?

Her voice was softer than it was on that first day.

She knew the answer.

I wanted to nod again and tell her:

Yeah, that's right. You know.

But instead I shrugged and kept walking. Walking until even though I couldn't see her, I was sure what she was going to do.

I stopped. Breathed. And slowly looked back over my shoulder, trying to appear as calm and nonchalant as possible.

I'm not sure but I think one corner of her mouth jerked up before her friends could see.

A smile.

For me.

She lifted her powerful bony fist and stuck her beautiful finger up at me.

It felt more like a salute than a dismissal.

The actors laughed and went back to half dancing to their window music.

Playing with each other's hair.

Lighting each other's cigarettes.

But she stood apart. Watching me look at her.

A diamond. A sapphire.

In the rough.

All the way home, my chest burned like the candy fireball had moved into my heart.

The next day she was waiting for me again.

Whatyoulookinat?

This time, it sounded like she was happy to see me.

Her actors laughed and pointed at my skinny legs.

But she just smirked as usual and struck a pose.

Raised her finger at me.

She put her cigarette to her mouth and kissed it. Then blew the smoke-kiss in my direction.

I breathed in deep, as if I could suck it in.

It was the same the day after. And every day the following week, too.

I always walked real slow as soon as I caught sight of her and before she caught sight of me.

I'd stay on my side of the street and pretend not to notice her and her dancers, and they'd wait and pretend not to notice me, too.

She always waited until I was almost past them.

Whatyoulookinat?

Her voice was deep and smoky sexy.

I'd shrug and hope my voice wouldn't crack, but manage a quiet, *Nothin'.*

Then she'd say, *Yeah, right.*

As soon as my back was to her, I'd take five paces before I turned around so she could flash me a quick fireball smile.

Then flip me off.

I'd nod, like I knew it was a compliment.

The actors would laugh and dance faster.

She would smoke.

And I would walk home happy.

She was always smoking. Always smoking and waiting. For me.

That's how it was with us.

III.

It's November now, and the last week before Thanksgiving break. I won't see her for a while.

I wonder if she knows our days are numbered.

I wonder if she cares.

When I get to her street, I pause and listen for the window music. The voices.

I walk more slowly the minute I hear her name.

Her friends elbow each other to look my way.

Here comes your boyfriend, Sapphie.

Her cigarette hangs loosely from her fingers, as if she wants to let go but can't.

Our eyes meet on purpose for the first time.

I let my mouth turn up the way hers does for me.

When she sees, she laughs.

You poor puppy.

As soon as she says it, it is exactly how I feel.

Like a puppy whose master told him to "stay" while he walked away.

That's me. Standing on my side of the street watching her like I am some sad dog.

I feel my hound-dog eyes droop with dejection.

She seems to wait to make sure no one else is watching before she lets the left corner of her mouth perk up.

She juts out her chin the way she does.

Whatyoulookinat?

She brings her cigarette to her mouth but doesn't put it in.

She watches me and waits.

She flicks the tip with her pinkie and ashes fly from her hand like magic stardust.

Yo!

You gonna answer me?

I startle at the sound of these new words and how they sound from her mouth.

My stomach dances.

I suck in the air and imagine I am tasting her smoke from over here on my side of the street.

I hold it in my chest, and it burns like that candy fireball trapped in my heart.

You, I say, sending the heat back her way.

Her friends crack up, but she steps forward.

My chest, my heart, my everything glows like the embers on her cigarette, waiting for her response.

She steps forward, expressionless.

But her eyes are sapphires.

Ha!

She barks the word at me, then takes a cool, long drag and lifts her chin higher in my direction.

She eyes me up and down in her usual, wonderful, awful way.

I try to look taller.

Slowly, her lips bloom and open into a real smile as she gives me the finger.

I lift my chin back at her and feel my own finger go up.

She crosses her arms and nods approvingly.

But she doesn't wave me over to her side of the street.

I know now that she never will.

I don't fit on her stage.

Just like she doesn't fit on mine.

Not at school. Not on this side of the street.

The heat seeps out of me.

I didn't want this good-bye.

But Sapphire is standing there watching me.

Waiting for me to move on.

I nod and turn away.

I walk down my side of the street, feeling her eyes on me as the distance grows between us.

You, I want to say again, even though she already knows it.

I was always lookinat you.

But instead I just keep walking.

IV.

I don't look back when I turn the corner and walk the next block.

She's out of sight now. Gone.

That's what I'm thinking when I step into the street without waiting for the cross signal.

That's what I'm thinking when the car hits me.

I don't feel anything.

I just hear the thud.

My body twists in a way I didn't know it could. Then gray pavement rushes at me.

For some reason I don't think *pavement,* though.

I think *asphalt.*

That's what my grandfather calls it.

I reach out with my hands and feel the roughness of it as my hands slide across with the rush of my fall.

Then my face hits.

Scrapes.

The asphalt is surprisingly warm for a November day.

I lie there, thinking about this. About my face. On the warm asphalt.

And how it is slowly starting to feel wet.

When I glance around, I think I am looking through a tunnel.

But then I realize I am looking through the bottom of a car.

I can see all the pipes and rusty metal parts.

A door opens. The metal creaks.

I wonder how old the car is. Probably as old as my grandfather's clunker.

Small clear and yellow shards of plastic rain down on me in tiny diamond shapes. Like a broken stained-glass window.

I study them, thinking, *headlight.*

That's a funny name.

I roll away from the car and peer up at the sky.

It isn't blue today. It's gray. Maybe a little green.

How many shades of blue and gray can the sky be?

I wonder if the choices are infinite or if there is a set number.

A head blocks my view.

It is a man's head and he is peering down at me with curiosity, as if I am some sort of roadkill he's never seen before.

Me, a rare bird.

Not Nobody.

I blink.

He blinks.

"Wha—?" I start to say.

"You're OK," he answers.

He has brown eyes and a beard. Trimmed. Odd. With a little patch under his bottom lip.

A goatee gone wrong. I've seen it before. At school.

194

The janitor, I think.

And then Nate's words, *soul patch,* and I think how funny that sounds, too. A patch of soul.

I tell myself I need to remember this. The details.

So I can tell the police in case I die.

I laugh, realizing if I die I won't be able to tell them anything.

The janitor keeps pacing back and forth, not taking his eyes off me.

The broken plastic crunches under his feet, and he swears with each step.

Shit, he mutters.

Shit, shit, shit.

He stops and stands over me again.

His head sways above me. I can't tell if he is actually swaying or if I am just dizzy.

"Am I OK?" I ask him.

You're just a deer, he says quietly.

"Huh?"

Shit.

He walks away.

The car door creaks shut.

Tires turn close to my face.

I squeeze my eyes closed, waiting for him to finish the job.

Nothing happens.

I blink again as the pain I know was on its way hits.
Hard.

It starts with the stinging on my face.

Then a strange sharpness in my legs that I've never felt before.

I don't move, just let the pain spread through my body.

There was a car.

And it hit me.

There was a man with an annoying beard.

The janitor from school.

But he took off.

The side of my face is on the asphalt.

No. Pavement.

I might be dead.

No. If I was dead, I wouldn't be thinking, *I'm dead.* Or be able to feel this . . . pain.

There's a stinging from my palm to my elbow. It scrapes against the pavement as I try to roll over.

I stop trying.

"Are you all right?"

I try to turn my head toward the voice.

Someone is leaning over me again.

A girl this time.

196

With the sun behind her, I mostly just see her silhouette.

The sunlight behind her is like a halo.

And now I do wonder if I'm dead.

The angel bends down.

"Jesus. That's gotta hurt."

Would an angel say *Jesus*?

"Can you move?"

She touches my shoulder. It is the only thing that doesn't sting or stab.

She reaches out her hands to help me sit up. They feel tiny in mine. Like a little kid's.

But now that I can see her face, I know she is not one.

She is Claire Harris from school.

The object of countless discussions between me and Nate.

I can hear Nate's voice in my head now.

Dude, Claire Harris just touched you.

I wait for the new pain to settle down again.

And think of Nate and his broken middle finger.

And how he's Finger Boy now.

But I am still Nobody.

Except that I'm the one staring at Claire Harris.

A small dog sniffs my elbow.

This has to be a dream.

She is like Dorothy from *The Wizard of Oz*.

With Toto.

I look down, expecting to see a yellow brick road.

Maybe I'm dead after all.

Claire helps me stand.

This must mean I didn't break every bone in my legs.

Also, not dead.

The little dog dances anxiously around us.

"I'm just gonna walk home now," I say shakily.

"Are you sure you're OK?" Claire asks.

I jerk my head down the street. "Yeah. It's not far."

"We'll walk with you. Just in case."

The dog yips.

Just in case what?

I test my cardboard legs.

They work.

We walk.

"How bad does it hurt?" She gestures toward my scraped-up arms.

I imagine one of those ridiculous face charts the doctor gives you.

"Cry face," I say.

Claire laughs. "My doctor uses those charts too."

"Mine always doubts me," I say. "She thinks I'm a wimp."

"Well, I think today would be an exception."

She gestures to the small rivulets of blood running down my arm.

Not gushing, but enough to make me look tough.

I wish Sapphie could see me.

Tough like this.

Like her.

"Are you sure you're OK?" Claire asks. "Maybe we should call your parents?"

That is the last thing I want to do.

They will want to take me to the hospital.

And my grandfather will want to come.

It will all be very dramatic in the way that nothing normally is in our house.

They will ask questions.

They will fuss.

And my grandfather will start to cry.

And that will make my parents cry.

Because he's so old and sad.

Claire smiles at me.

"I have some tissues in my bag. We should mop up some of that blood."

We stop walking and face each other.

I wonder who she sees.

The real me?

Or some stage version of me.

The little dog sniffs my leg.

"This is Oliver," Claire says.

Instead of a collar, he has a pink belt tied around his neck. It's attached to a yellow belt to make a leash.

"I just got him today."

He wags his stump of a tail.

"Hi," I say.

Claire reaches into her bag and scrounges around, then pulls out a mini tissue pack and a bottle of water.

"You have a lot of stuff in there," I tell her.

"I like to be prepared," she says.

For what?

She opens the bottle and pours a few drops of water onto the tissue.

She dabs it gently against the scrape that runs all they way up my arm.

It stings and tickles at the same time.

I try not to flinch.

I try to enjoy this moment.

Claire Harris touching me, *nursing* me.

What would Finger Boy say?

She finishes cleaning me up, and we start walking again.

Oliver trots in front of us, his pink-yellow belt-leash swinging back and forth.

It feels natural.

As if we've always done this.

I try to imagine Sapphie here, by my side.

Whatyoulookinat? she'd ask.

You.

But then what?

Would we share a cigarette?

Go hang out with the actors?

What if all we ever had was *Whatyoulookinat?*

And the finger?

"You're bleeding again." Claire gestures toward my arm. "And you're limping. C'mon."

She takes my arm very gently and leads me to the steps of an apartment building.

For the first time, I feel the cold November air around us.

Claire gets out her water and tissues again.

"You're going to have to go to the hospital, I think."

"No, it'll stop bleeding." I press more tissues against my cuts and hope I'm right.

Oliver watches, his ears perked up at us.

My neck has started to ache.

My head, too.

And my legs.

Then I feel like I'm going to throw up.

I get up too fast and almost fall down. Cardboard legs again.

"Going. To be. Sick," I say, trying to steady myself.

I rush down the steps to some low bushes and lose the contents of my stomach.

I cringe at the sounds I make.

I can barely stand up, I'm so dizzy.

Finally I drop to my knees and hang on to a branch.

"Oh my God," Claire says. "You must have a concussion!"

"No," I say.

"I should call someone." She pulls out her phone.

"No," I say again. "Please. My parents—"

But what?

My parents what?

Will overreact.

Baby me.

Freak out.

Worry.

And my grandfather will cry.

"I'll call my mom. She'll know what to do. She used to be a nurse."

She helps me back over to the steps, and I sip from the water bottle.

It's almost empty.

Claire walks away from me to make the call.

Claire Harris just saw me puke my guts out.

Finger Boy would laugh. I wouldn't blame him.

"My mom's coming to get us," Claire says as she walks back over to me and sits down again.

"Today has been a crazy day," she says.

I nod.

But then I wonder if she means for her or me.

"First, I ditch school for the first time."

"Really?"

"Yeah. I'm a very boring person, it turns out."

Really?

"Then I kind of inherit Oliver from a homeless woman."

Oliver barks.

"Then I find you, hit by a car!"

She shakes her head. "Crazy."

"So you said."

"Because it is."

I can't argue.

Claire glances down the street, then lifts her face to the setting sun.

She breathes in the cool air as if it's something to taste.

As if this whole situation is something to drink in.

Then she looks at me and smiles.

Not like the girl on the wall.

Not with a jutted-out chin.

Not like I don't belong.

Or shouldn't get too close.

Just natural. Not romantic. But like a friend.

Like someone true. It feels like she is seeing the real me, and I am seeing the real her.

Not *Claire Harris.*

Just Claire Harris.

And by seeing each other that way, we're seeing our own true selves, too.

All the stinging, all the aching, all the dizziness, seems to melt away.

Just for a moment.

This is me, I think. And I swear I can hear her think the same thing.

"It feels like this was meant to happen, don't you think?" she asks.

The funny thing is,

I do.

SEVEN:
APE BOY
(Dylan: 3:10 p.m.)

I.

MY BACKPACK FEELS HEAVY AGAINST my legs as we drive through the city. It feels heavier than it ever has, even though I've been carrying this thing for days. I know it probably seems crazy that I'm carrying a brick around. It doesn't even make all that much sense to me. But once I stole it, I felt different. Like suddenly I was armed. Just in case I needed it. Until today, I had no idea what that would even mean.

It's not really a brick. It's a paver. You know, the gray cement kind that's supposed to look like a stone that you line a garden bed with? Or a driveway? I stole it from our neighbors. They hate me. All summer they're on me about our lawn and me getting around to mowing it. And all fall they're on me about how I need to rake the leaves. The only time I get any sort of break is a few months during the winter if we're lucky enough to get some snow to cover up the mess. It's rare. And we all know what's underneath.

My neighbors are what my friends would call douches. Both the dad and the son. I haven't decided which of them is worse. The son is sort of like a bigger, grosser, meaner version of his dad. He is an ape. Everything his dad says, he says. His dad calls me a lazy ass; he calls me a lazy ass. His dad calls me a little bitch; he calls me a little bitch. What does that even mean? Do they think I'm gay? A pussy? What?

My mom tells me to ignore them. She tells me there is more to life than a tidy yard. Her famous saying to her friends is "Love me, love my mess." She doesn't have many friends, but she has a brilliant mess.

My mom likes messes. Whenever we travel, which is almost never these days, she says she has to mess up the hotel room in order to be able to sleep. She always leaves housekeeping a twenty when we check out. I don't think it's enough.

When I was little, I never realized that not everyone couldn't see their living-room floor. Or didn't know the original color of the tile on the bathroom wall. When my dad left and never came back, I was too young to realize why. But now I have a pretty good guess.

When my sister, Sammy, and I figured out we were different, we also figured out how to cope. Mainly we didn't invite anyone over. We taught ourselves how to do laundry and how to keep our mom out of our rooms, as best we could. We learned to make sure to eat all the takeout so there are absolutely no leftovers. Leftovers end up in the stuffed, stinking refrigerator. No one is allowed to throw anything away that's in there unless it is completely empty. Sometimes when she's not home, we sneak stuff out. But we have to be careful, or she'll notice and get upset. Panic. Yell.

Mostly our mom is really nice. But things can set her off. Things can upset her. When that happens, she disappears down the narrow hall through her maze of boxes and bags full of outgrown clothes she won't part with and into her room. Her den. Her *cave*. Where she is surrounded by even more piles and piles and piles of stuff. Since I can remember, she has been building it around her. Someday she will disappear. That's my biggest fear.

So whenever I can, I sneak away bags and bins and boxes as stealthily as she sneaks them in. It's a balancing act neither of us talks about. But despite how frustrated she gets with me when she suspects I've taken something, my mother loves me. And I love her.

But I don't necessarily love her mess.

Sammy pretends she can't see my mother's piles of stuff. That she can't see the stacks of debris that separate her feet from the real floor. The minute she gets home from her cheerleading ridiculousness, she goes straight to her immaculate room and shuts the door. I hear her on the other side, going through her nightly routine. Logging on to her computer, talking with friends, singing to some crappy boy band while she does her homework. She lives in a perfectly pristine bubble.

It drives my mom crazy, but she is not allowed in Sammy's room. That's their agreement. I swear if my mom pauses in Sammy's doorway too long and gets a good look inside her clean, spacious room, she gets the sweats. That's why, most often, Sammy's door is shut. And locked.

My neighbors know one of their pavers is missing. From a crack in my window blind, I watched the dad walk out of his house to get the paper the morning after I stole it. He called Ape Boy outside to look at the small but gaping hole in their otherwise perfect driveway border. A chink in their armor. That's what it felt like, pulling it from the soil. Like I made a dent in their pristine fortress. Me. It felt good.

They weren't happy when they discovered the gaping hole. They both looked up at my house at the same time, knowing it must have been me. I stepped back from the window and pulled the paver out of my backpack and wondered if I'd gone too far. I was just so tired of the two of them calling me *bitch* and me not knowing what they meant. Tired of them telling me what a slob my mom is. And tired of them looking at my sister like they want to eat her. And I do mean that in the grossest way possible. But mostly, and I really hate even talking about this at all. I hate how Sammy seems to know and doesn't care. Sometimes I even think she likes it.

So I guess I do know why I picked up that paver. Because I knew it would piss them off. And because for some strange reason, having a piece of their perfect— knowing I could just take it—felt good. And I carry it now, just in case. Just in case I need to do something about those looks they give my sister. This might make me sound sexist and old-fashioned, feeling like I have to defend her honor, but that's not it. It's them. It's their disgusting faces. I know I would never really *do* anything. But I would like to scare them. I would like to scare the crap out of them. Smash their windshield, throw the brick through their newly washed living-room window. Or . . . I don't know. Just make a bigger chink.

I've seen the Apes slide the curtains back from their living room window when Sammy walks down the driveway. I've watched her wiggle her bum, giving them a show. She thinks it's funny. I do not. Because knowing the Apes, she is the one they think about and fantasize about when they . . . do things guys do.

My mom says all men are like that, "except you, Dyl." Like this is supposed to make it all OK.

I say to her, "Aren't you worried that someday they might try something?"

And she says, "Like what?"

As if she doesn't know.

"Sammy knows how to take care of herself," she says. And she and Sammy nod like they know something I don't.

"Do you *like* them looking at you?" I ask Sammy.

She tells me to shut up.

She's so mean to me sometimes. But I guess that's her role as my big sister. I know she loves me, even though she pretends not to know me. Even though she pretends that she doesn't live in this mess. Even though she lives in a fantasy world of clean, crisp cheerleading uniforms, basketball victories, and best friends who have never stepped foot in our house and don't know our secret. She cares. I see it in her eyes when she turns to look at me apologetically before she shuts her bedroom door and locks it. She needs her piece of perfect, too.

But I can't stop worrying about Sammy and the Apes. I have seen them watching her with their hungry ape-y eyes. And finally, today, all my worst fears came true.

We were at Little Cindy's, as usual. Me, Cal, and Jack. Normally we use the drive-thru, but there was a huge line, so we decided to go in. I saw him right away. He was pacing behind the counter, shouting orders at the other workers. When he saw me, he kind of shoved one of them aside and stood behind the register, waiting for us. He looked tough, even with his blue Little Cindy's polo and his stupid visor.

"What do you want, boys?" he asked us. He said *boys* like he meant something gross. Like we were worse than dog poo you step in with new shoes.

When I handed him my money, he grabbed my hand and squeezed it. The guys weren't paying attention. I tried to pull away, but Ape Boy is apelike in more ways than one. He's one of those guys who "goes to the gym." He wears these ridiculous black sweatpants and tank tops all the time. That's his other uniform. To show how buff he is. Gym. Job. I wonder what he hopes comes next, if anything. Maybe he just plans to mooch off his dad forever. Who knows?

But there he was, squeezing the hell out of my hand and giving me this look like he was going to eat *me*. He leaned forward and smiled this disgusting smile and said, really quiet, so only I could hear, "I had your sister."

He nodded his head in this satisfying way, then licked his lips. "And she liked it."

I didn't believe him. She wouldn't. He's Ape Boy. He's hairy. He's stupid. He's . . . *Ape Boy*. The guy who calls me *bitch*. She *wouldn't*.

He was just daring me to prove him wrong.

I played it cool, even though I felt like I was going to throw up.

"Right," I said. "Hope you had fun." Then I yanked my hand away and walked out of there. The guys grabbed my food for me. They didn't ask what was wrong. They know Ape Boy is always on my case. They try to make me feel better by telling me how he is working at Little Cindy's, for God's sake. So what do I care? He's a nobody.

I ate my food. Went back to school. I let the paver bruise my back as it thudded against me with each step. Felt the pain and knew it was time. The moment I knew would come was here: Ape Boy had gone too far. And now I was going to use their piece of perfect to make them pay.

ı | | ı

The boys in the car are quiet now. I can tell they're worried. We don't keep secrets from each other. Not in theory, anyway. But I suspect each of us has plenty. Everyone does, right?

"Where are we going, anyway?" Cal finally asks. We've been driving around for a while. No music. No questions. Just the Three Musketeers, aka us, looking out the window, wondering what finally caused me to lose my mind.

"Boulevard," I say. He nods and we continue on.

Cal glances over at me and raises his eyebrows in a silent *You OK?* kind of way.

I turn back to my window and squeeze the strap of my backpack. My back aches against the seat behind me. I'm sure the bruise is purple by now. A perfect rectangular shape.

I picture Ape Boy again, grinning about "doing" my sister. I shouldn't believe him. I should go to her and tell her what he said. But I barely ever see her alone because she's always hiding in her bubble. Or avoiding me at school. Or at practice. Or at away games. I realize I hardly even know her anymore.

Once I caught her smiling at Ape Boy. He was washing his car. He'd tossed his tank top on the grass. He had a tan where his shirt should be. He nodded at her but didn't say hi. She smiled back that way girls do when they know you think they're hot. Like they know you've checked them out and the smile says, *It's OK*, without really knowing what that means. What if she's drawn to their immaculate lawn? Their probably spotless house? Their lack of clutter?

I feel the outside of my backpack and find the shape of the paver. Squeeze it.

"Yo, D. Now where?"

I look out my window at the strip malls and food chains and boarded-up shops that used to rent XXX movies or fix appliances or sell flowers until I spot the Little Cindy's sign up ahead. The little girl in pigtails looms over the parking lot.

"Leave me at Little Cindy's," I say.

Cal grunts. "Yeah, right. We're not leaving you anywhere."

"Why do you want to go there?" Jack asks. He's always the practical one.

"Just go," I say.

"D., you seem kinda freaked out. Maybe you should tell us what's up before you do something stupid." Cal gives me a concerned look. Even though he's in the back, I can tell Jack is making the same face.

"Forget it," I say. "I'll jump out at the next light."

"Relax. I'll take you," Cal says.

We pull into the lot, and Cal shuts off the engine. They wait for me to get out first

"You're not taking that, are you?" Jack asks.

I don't answer. I open my door and swing the bag over my shoulder. It thuds heavily against my bruised back.

The lot is pretty full for the afternoon, and we have to weave our way through the parked cars. When we get near the last row, there's something familiar about the car at the end. As I look closer, I notice a headlight's broken. I wonder if it's the car we crammed earlier, but what are the chances? I keep walking. The guys follow me.

I open the door and we're engulfed by the smell that is uniquely Little Cindy's. There's a long line of the afterschool crowd waiting to torture the register workers. Ape Boy is behind the counter, talking to a girl cashier with long dark hair. He's looking at her the same way he looks at Sammy, the bastard.

"Well?" Cal asks. "Who's getting the brick?"

Jack elbows him. "No one!"

Cal scopes the place out curiously, then sees where I'm looking. "That guy again? Your asshole neighbor? What's with you two?"

The brick presses against my back. I clench my teeth and force myself to breathe through my nose, slowly, to calm my racing heart. I imagine myself waiting patiently in line, stepping forward as each customer takes a tray and moves on. Inch by inch until it's my turn. I will order food I will never eat. Then I will slip my backpack off my shoulder and onto the floor, pretending I need to get my wallet out of it. But instead, I will reach for the gray paver. I will grip it tightly and raise it up so he sees it clearly. He will say something stupid. Last words almost always are. Something like, *Hey, that's my dad's paver!* And everyone will look over at us. And I will say something equally stupid because the one thing I didn't plan on was a good one-liner to deliver just before I make him eat it. So I'll say something really lame, like, *This is for my sister!* And then I'll wind up and take aim and—

"Uh-oh," Cal says, grabbing Jack's shirt. "Isn't that the guy from this morning?"

He's right. It's the guy in the Taurus who we ripped off.

"Crap," Jack says. "We need to get out of here."

Cal nods. "Act normal."

He leads and Jack follows. But I hesitate, my eyes still fixed on Ape Boy, who sees me and nods cockily in my direction, then licks his lips. My hands form fists. I've never really felt this way before. I've never wanted to *hurt* someone before. I want to punch his mouth so it hurts to lick his lips. I don't care about the brick anymore. I want to use my fist. I want to feel the contact—

Taurus man stands up, recognizing me. I look from him to Ape Boy. I can't move.

Jack comes back just in time. He grabs my backpack, still over my shoulder, and drags me out the door. We hurry to Cal's car and get the hell out of there. As we race out of the parking lot, Taurus Man stands behind the glass door, giving us the finger. I could swear he is crying. I am filled with guilt.

I lean my head against the headrest and close my eyes.

What is wrong with us?

What is wrong with me?

II.

"Did you see who Taurus Man was with?" Jack asks. "Stephen, from school. He's in our lit. elective."

"Who cares?" Cal says. "What's he going to do?"

But he says it in a way that convinces no one. I hope this means our scamming days are over, though I wouldn't mind pulling a fast one on Ape Boy and his father.

"Plans foiled, I guess. Huh, D.? So, where to now?"

I don't answer.

I wish Cal could be sincere for one minute of his life. I think calling me D. is his way of showing me that he thinks I'm special enough to him to have a nickname. But I just think it's stupid.

Cal shrugs and keeps driving. As always, we end up at Jack's and go out back to our tree house. Or hideout. Or whatever you want to call it. It sounds so babyish calling it a clubhouse, even though I guess that's basically what it is.

We sit in our usual places on the floor, and Cal pulls out the stash of *Playboy*s we've accumulated over the years. "I don't suppose either of you two bozos have some weed?" he asks.

As if. Any time one of us scores a joint, it's gone within hours.

I turn on some music from the ancient boom box we got at a yard sale while Jack starts dealing out cards. When there's nothing else to do, and there's not enough to talk about, we play Texas Hold 'em. We keep an old Quaker Quick Oats container full of pennies that we use for the game. Jack doles out twenty-five to each of us. No one keeps the pennies at the end. They go back in the Quaker box. Someone, most likely Cal, drew a huge boob next to the Quaker guy's face on the package so his smile makes him look like a sleazy pervert instead of some nice old guy trying to encourage kids to eat a nutritious breakfast.

My first hand is a two of hearts and a three of spades. Typical. Cal raises immediately like he always does, and Jack and I fold as usual. My backpack is next to me. I reach over and feel the paver inside. I'm sure they notice, but no one says anything.

My next hand is a five of clubs and a nine of diamonds. I fold again. Cal raises, but this time Jack calls. Jack only ever calls when he has a really good hand, so Cal and Jack check and call the rest of the hand. When they flip, Jack has a pair of queens and Cal has a six and ten of spades.

"If I win the next hand, D. gives me that brick and I get rid of it, no questions asked," says Cal. "If I win the whole game, he tells us exactly what the hell he was going to do with it."

"I'm in," Jack says. "For your own good," he adds, giving me an apologetic look.

"D.?" Cal asks. "You in?"

"Do I have a choice?"

Cal looks at Jack and shrugs. "Doesn't look like it." He smirks and tosses a bunch of pennies into the pot without even checking his hand.

I have a jack and a ten. "What did you just bet?" I ask. Cal shrugs and leaves it to Jack to count.

"Eleven," Jack says.

I slide my pennies to the middle of the plywood floor. Cal studies me for tells. I try to give him my blank face, but it's impossible. We all know each other too well.

"D. has something good," Cal says. He bites his bottom lip.

Jack calls and slides his pennies into the pot with mine. Then he acts as dealer and sets the first three cards down. A ten, a queen, and a nine of hearts. Cal checks. A rarity.

I throw in five more pennies. I have a pair and could get a straight. Jack folds. I smirk, even though I know in poker that's a big no-no.

"You know I'm gonna win," Cal says. "Just fold and save your pennies." He tosses in five to call.

Jack flips an ace. I study the cards and think of all the scenarios in which Cal could beat me. There are a lot. I tap my fingers on the floor as I decide what to do. I only have ten pennies left. I throw in five.

Cal calls, and Jack flips over an eight of diamonds.

This time Cal smirks. I grin too. I've got a straight.

"Let's see 'em, boys," Jack says.

I flip mine first. "Nice hand." Jack nods approvingly.

We turn to Cal. He makes a big deal out of slowly revealing his cards. First card, a king of hearts. I'm safe. Then he slowly turns the other card over. Jack of hearts.

"Dang!" Jack says. "What are the chances?"

I'm starting to wonder.

Cal makes a big show of sliding all the pennies in front of him and making little piles of ten. When he's done, he looks up, as if he didn't realize we were watching and waiting.

"There," he says. "OK, D., hand it over."

"What?"

"The brick." He reaches for my backpack, but I pull it away.

They wait.

"Fine." I unzip my bag and lift out the paver. It feels a lot heavier in my hand than on my back.

"So, what's it for?" Cal asks. "Exactly."

"You have to win the whole game to find out," I say. "Remember?"

"You're a little creepy, D. I have to admit, I'm getting bad vibes." He places the paver in the center of our circle.

"Heavy," Jack says.

"Surprisingly," Cal adds.

"Are you OK?" Jack asks.

A trickle of sweat runs down my temple to my jaw.

"Yeah," I say. "Fine."

"'Cause it's November and it's cold and you're kind of sweating a lot," Jack says.

"I'm fine," I say again.

Cal rubs his hands together. "Next hand!"

Jack starts shuffling. I watch carefully to make sure he isn't doing something sketchy with the cards. It just seems too lucky for Cal to have won that last hand.

I wait until all the cards are passed out before I touch mine, for good luck. We all follow the same rule. Sometimes I even wait for everyone else to pick up theirs before I touch mine, for extra luck, even though that hasn't worked out for me so far.

I have five pennies left and another lousy hand. A nine of clubs and a six of hearts. I fold.

Cal and Jack throw in their five. Cal raises. Typical. Jack folds. He has even fewer pennies than me now. Cal is going to win.

Next hand, I get a seven and a king, both hearts. Could be worse.

Cal calls and Jack goes all in with his four remaining pennies. Since we're all bet up, Jack starts to turn all five cards up. A three of aces, a nine of hearts, a queen of hearts. He pauses. The right side of Cal's mouth twitches. This is a tell I have no idea the meaning of. One more heart and I'll be in great shape. Jack flips the next card and it's a two of hearts. Yes! I have this. I can feel it.

The last card is an ace of spades.

Jack's the first to show his cards, even though it should be me. Two tens.

I flip mine.

"Ooh! Nice hand," Jack says. "That's gonna be hard to beat."

"Hard," Cal says. "But not impossible." He flips his cards over. Four of hearts and ace of hearts.

"No way!" I say.

Cal shrugs. "You know I'm lucky."

I shake my head.

Cal picks up the paver and passes it from one hand to the other. "So, D. What were you planning on doing with this thing, anyway?"

Jack gathers the pennies nervously and puts them back in the container.

The image from my fantasy comes to mind again.

Me: Winding up with the paver in my hand.

Ape Boy: A look of confusion, surprise, and terror on his face, cowering.

Me: *This is for my sister!*

But that's about as far as I get in the fantasy. I can't even make myself *imagine* smashing Ape Boy's head.

"Nuh-nothing," I say. "Actually."

"Right. You have to tell us. That was the bet."

"I just told you. Nothing. I don't know. Maybe I just wanted to scare someone. All right?"

"Who?" Cal asks. "The jerk from Little Cindy's?"

"Dewey Hartson," Jack says. "Your neighbor, right?"

"How'd you know his name?" I ask.

"Name tag. All the employees have to wear 'em."

It's strange how I never think of Dewey as anyone but Ape Boy. *Dewey* just doesn't fit. *Dewey* sounds like the kid everyone beats up in middle school, not the perv who makes gross gestures to the girl next door.

"Why did you want to kill him with the paver?" Cal asks seriously.

"I didn't want to kill him."

"Why'd you want to *scare* him?" Jack asks.

"I don't want to talk about it."

"A bet's a bet!" Cal says, way too cheerfully.

"The bet was I'd tell you what I was going to do with it. Not why."

He bounces the paver from hand to hand. "Just tell us what he did. Maybe we'll want to kill him ourselves. Maybe we'll do it for you."

"Where'd you get that thing, anyway?" Jack asks. "Did you steal it?"

Jack is the only one who's been to my house and gone inside. He's the only one who knows what my real life is like. Cal pulls to the curb when he picks me up and drops me off. Sure, he knows our yard is a wreck, but he has no clue what the house is like on the inside. The only reason Jack does is because I screwed up one time and overslept, and he came to the door to get me. My mom, being somewhat clueless, invited him in. She brought him to my room, and I remember waking up to see a look of horror and shock on his face. My room isn't so bad, but he had to walk through the house to get there. Also, since my mom ran out of space to put stuff, a lot of times she puts boxes in my room "temporarily." She always promises to move them, but it only happens when I do it secretly while she sleeps. I know there's a name for what she does. But I don't think it's as bad as the stories you see on TV.

Jack seemed to think so, though. Later that day, he asked me what it was like to live with all that stuff. But he said *stuff* like he meant filth. I told him my mom needed it, so we put up with it. He seemed to understand. We never talked about it again after that. But any time I overslept, he waited outside. That's how he knows about the Apes. Because a few weeks ago he was waiting for me and when I came to the door, they were outside, washing Ape Boy's car.

"That your girlfriend, bitch?" Ape Boy called.

We stood and looked at them, with their Turtle Wax and buffing cloths and wifebeater shirts and black sweatpants and plastic sandals even though it was cold out. Then we looked at each other and laughed.

In hindsight, it probably wasn't the best reaction. Bullies do not like to be laughed at. But Cal isn't exactly small, so when the Apes started walking toward us and Cal got out of the car and it was suddenly three against two, the Apes stopped in their tracks and waited for us to leave. Anyone checking the scene, their scene, would have been blinded by the shine on the blue muscle car. Or the meticulous gray driveway lined with matching pavers to divide the edge of their driveway from their immaculate lawn. I swear, Ape Man tiptoes across the grass every time a leaf falls on it to pick it up as quickly as possible. So we walked on and got in the car, and Cal peeled away from the curb, leaving skid marks on the street in front of the Apes' house just to piss them off. It was kind of beautiful, really.

"So what did he do?" Jack asks.

"Who?" I ask, pretending to be clueless.

"Must have been bad!" Cal points to my earlobe with

his index finger. "Your ear's turning red. It only does that when you're pissed or have a bad hand."

"You realize you just gave away my tell?"

"Crap. Jack, forget what I just said."

"So, what did your neighbor the Little Cindy's guy do to deserve a smashed-in face?" Jack asks, gesturing toward the paver.

They wait.

I sigh and breathe in the stagnant tree-house air. Even in the November cold, it's nasty.

"He just . . . went too far. That's all. Can we drop it now?"

"Um . . . no? We want to know what he did!" Cal leans forward as if I'm going to tell him a secret. Whatever.

"He made a comment about Sammy," I say. "It was stupid. But . . . just knowing that guy even looks at her makes me want to . . ." I make a fist.

"Aw, what a good brother," Cal says approvingly. "God, she's hot."

"Seriously?" I ask. "Shut up."

"Well, she *is*," Cal says. "You can't really deny that. But I'm with you. Sammy in that guy's dirty thoughts is very wrong and must be stopped."

"Agreed," Jack says.

Cal reaches for the brick. "Give me that thing."

"Forget it," I say. "I'm not doing anything. He's lying, anyway."

"Whoa, what do you mean, 'lying'? What did he tell you?"

Crap. I didn't mean to say that out loud.

"Nothing."

"Right. You think we'll let you off without the details now?" Cal asks. "Please tell me he didn't say he touched her."

"Worse," I say.

"C'mon, he has to be lying," Jack says.

"He said they did it." I zero in on the paver. Suddenly I have a renewed desire to smash it in Ape Boy's face. Now that I've said the words out loud, the possibility of them being together seems even more awful.

"Gross," Cal says. "And also? No way. Sammy's way too smart and cool. The only way they did it is if he slipped her something and she was completely passed out."

"That's helpful," I say.

But actually, it's better than imagining her doing it willingly. I feel like hell for thinking that, but it would be the only logical reason she would ever go near him. In either scenario, I would still want to kill him.

"Look. It's obvious the dude is lying. He's just trying to

get your goat." Cal reaches for his backpack and scrounges around inside. He pulls out a Milky Way bar and takes a huge bite. The room instantly smells like chocolate.

My stomach growls loudly, and Cal hands me the bar. His teeth marks show on the end of it. "No thanks," I say, passing it over to Jack.

He takes a bite. "So, what are you going to do?"

"Nothing," I say. "Nothing with that, anyway."

"Are you going to tell Sammy he's been spreading lies about her?" Cal asks. "I bet Jacob would love that."

"He's not her boyfriend. He just follows her around and lusts after her like everyone else."

"What about the paver?" Cal asks.

"I'm keeping it. It's the only thing I've ever stolen in my life, and I'm not giving it back. Besides, they already replaced it."

Cal shakes his head and grabs what's left of the Milky Way back from Jack. "Those guys have an unhealthy obsession with their curb appeal. Just saying."

"It's all they have," I say.

It's a big realization, actually. I think maybe it really *is* all they have. I have no idea where Mrs. Ape is, if there ever was one. And Ape Boy never seems to bring any girls home. So who are they trying to impress? Are their postage-stamp-size house and their stupid muscle car and truck the only things they have? The only things besides each other? Ape Boy has a crap job. I don't know what Ape Man does. Maybe they are just miserable. Maybe they are just clinging to the one thing they can control.

"D.? You still here?" Cal shakes me.

"Huh?" I look at the paver. Maybe I should give it back after all.

"I was saying I think we should keep the paver here," Cal says. "It's like . . . a monument."

"A monument to what?" I ask.

"To bravery. To sticking it to the assholes."

"Yeah," Jack says. "I like it. And . . . it's like you stuck it to them even better because you didn't *do* anything with it. They're probably waiting for you to, like, smash the windshield of their car or something. They're probably all freaked out, wondering when you'll strike."

But instead of making me feel better, that makes me feel worse. Sure, they call me a bitch. Sure, I have no idea what it means. Sure, Ape Boy lusts after my sister. But *everyone* does that. Maybe they're pissed because our crappy house is making their pristine one less shiny. Maybe they are just tired of doing all that work and watching me do nothing.

Cal gets up and puts the paver on the shelf we keep our "treasures" on: a photo of the three of us, a trophy our

230

Little League team won in the fifth grade, a two-dollar bill some old guy gave Jack for helping him find his cat, the quarter we flip on when we have to figure out whose turn it is to go to the house to get provisions, and Cal's sixth-grade report card with three As. They earned him thirty bucks from his mom. They were the last As he ever got.

"But this thing doesn't stand for something good," I tell them. "Don't put it there."

"Sure it does," Cal says. "It stands for . . . you keeping your cool. Yeah."

"Only because Taurus Man came after us and I didn't get a chance to do anything," I point out.

"You still wouldn't have done it," Jack says.

I can't deny it.

"It'll be our reminder," Cal says. "A symbol."

"Of what?" Jack asks.

"Of the day we stopped the road scam," Cal says.

We're all quiet.

"For real?" I ask.

"Yeah. Seeing that guy kind of freaked me out."

"I always hated it," Jack says.

"Me too," I say.

Cal reaches in his pocket and pulls out a wad of bills. He puts it under the brick. "Another reminder. We'll never spend this money. Got it? Now. Let's play another hand."

III.

We play cards for what feels like hours and no time at all, until it's too cold and dark to keep going. When Cal takes me home, there's a car at the curb and Sammy is standing next to it, leaning in. She appears to be yelling. She turns and squints at Cal's headlights, then goes back to yelling at whoever's inside. I get out and start toward her to make sure everything's OK.

"Just go!" she yells. "I never want to see or speak to you again! Ever! You're a *pig*!"

Jacob, the driver, says something I can't hear, then revs the engine and takes off.

"What's all that racket!" Ape Boy yells from his yard. He's standing outside, under their porch light. He's always standing out there at night, like he's patrolling the neighborhood or something.

"Are you OK?" I ask Sammy, ignoring him.

She's crying.

"Yeah, fine. Just . . . never mind. I'm fine."

She says it quietly and sadly, like all the fire she had a minute ago has turned to ash.

"Hey! I'm talking to you!" Ape Boy says.

Sammy rolls her eyes. "C'mon, let's go inside."

I wave Cal away, and he drives off.

Sammy and I start to walk up the overgrown path to our front door. The dead grass is as high as our knees and completely gone to seed. My mom made a path to the front door with different-colored carpet squares she got for free when she pretended to be looking to buy carpet at a local store. That was years ago when we were kids. The carpet was supposed to keep the weeds from growing up. Sammy and I used to jump from square to square, pretending they were islands and the grass around them was green acid that would burn our feet if we touched it.

Now we step on the squares again. They're so old and worn that weeds are growing up through them, and grass has grown so thick around them they barely make a path at all. Sammy hops from one square to another, just like when we were young. She's in her cheerleading outfit, and her skirt swishes like a little kid's with each jump.

I hop behind her. "Don't touch the acid!" I yell.

"Hey!" Ape Boy calls again.

Sammy stops and glances over at him.

He looks from me to her to me again. "You ever gonna mow that lawn, bitch?"

"Who are you calling a bitch?" Sammy asks.

"Me," I say. "But I don't get it."

"Leave my brother alone!" Sammy yells. It's the

233

first time I remember her standing up for me. I want to hug her.

Ape Boy makes a disgusted face at us, like we're trash. "You live in a dump!" he yells back.

Sammy smiles at me. We both crack up. What else can we do? We know we live in a dump. What's it to him?

"What a jerk," she says quietly. And I know for sure that everything he said was a lie.

"Love me, love my mess," Sammy quotes. She takes another hop, then looks over at Ape Boy in his pristine driveway. Slowly she lifts up her arm and gives him the finger. Then she hops all the way to the front door.

Before we go inside, I look over at Ape Boy one more time. He's just watching us. Not moving. Like he's suddenly completely lost.

Maybe no one has ever given him the finger before.

I can't believe it, but I suddenly feel a little sorry for him.

Instead of giving him the finger, I wave.

"Good night!" I call over as friendly as I can.

He shrugs and shakes his head in a confused way.

I smile and go inside.

EIGHT:
DIRTY FINGER
(Lacy: 4:05 p.m.)

I.

SHARP WORDS CUT THE STAGNANT BUS AIR. Shouts about who should sit where. The usual insults. I sit quietly and stare out the smudgy window, waiting for the Girls.

The heater under my seat blows blasts of hot air up my bare legs. The scum-green seat is prickly hot under my thighs. I pull at the hem of my skirt so it covers them up better, but I can still feel my sweat forming under my skin. I just hope when I get up, there won't be wet spots on the seat. *Please. Not that.*

I look down at my chest and the fuzzy red *I* sewn there. *I* for Irving High. Red on white. I remember when I first got it and tried it on. Staring at myself in the full-length mirror on the back of my bedroom door. How the folds at the waist wouldn't smooth out. Because it wasn't sweater folds; it was my stomach. My "spare tire," as my mother would say. My muffin top.

My mother opened my door without knocking, swinging mirror me aside. Her own image stood where I once did. She, of course, is slimmer. Taller. Better. I watched her eyes travel from my head, down to my chest, my stomach, my thighs. The disgust she didn't even try to hide.

"That costume doesn't suit you," she said, as if I was dressing for Halloween.

She sighed. She couldn't seem to take her eyes off my thighs. Was it old recognition? Did she remember when she looked like me? Even worse? Before she had her fat sucked out and stomach stapled over? Was she imagining doing the same to me? Now that the pain of surgery was a memory, she was always hinting about my "someday" future of thin. When I would have my thighs and stomach sucked and stapled if that's what it took, to slowly disappear. If only I was old enough.

When she finally met my eyes, she made her worried face. The one that predicted nothing good could come of me in this "costume."

"It's for cheerleading," I told her. "Remember? I made the squad."

236

Sometimes when I tell her things, I think I am waking her from a dream.

"Oh," she said. "I forgot."

I petted the soft sweater and swished the skirt a little.

"What will you do with your hair?" she asked.

"I want a French braid with a red ribbon. A lot of girls wear theirs that way. Can you do mine?"

"I don't know how."

That was a lie.

When I was little and chubby was still cherub-acceptable, she spent hours dressing me up as Little Miss Cute, braiding my hair, planting pretty bows on my head, making me wear shiny shoes.

"That's OK," I told her. "One of the Girls can do it, then."

She raised her right eyebrow. She always raises her right eyebrow when she doesn't believe me.

"Sammy," I said. "Or Grace or Claire."

The eyebrow remained poised. She still hadn't accepted my newfound friends. Hadn't accepted the fact that they existed. She's spent so long trying to get me to have girlfriends instead of "that Stephen boy," and now that I finally have some, she can't seem to break out of her cloud of negativity.

"You haven't had any of them over," she said. "So I wasn't sure how it was working out."

I haven't had any of them over because I don't want her comparing me to them. I don't want her asking me why all my friends are skinny and I'm not.

Because she would. I know she would.

"It's working out fine," I said. "If it weren't for them . . ." I paused. I didn't want to tell my mother that the Girls got me on the squad. That would raise suspicions of why. And even I didn't want to fully explore that.

"I wouldn't have tried out," I said vaguely.

She studied my face, maybe picturing what my hair would look like pulled back.

"You have such a pretty face," she said. *Such a shame about the rest of you,* she didn't need to say out loud.

That night I looked up how to braid my own hair on YouTube and practiced for hours until I got it right. Just in case the Girls couldn't do it after all.

I am careful not to cross my legs as I sit here, waiting for everyone to find a seat so we can go. Instead, I squeeze my knees together and try to move forward so that I am sitting on the edge of the seat. This helps keep my thighs from swelling out on the sides and accentuating my cellulite. My mother calls it "cottage cheese." I've seen her notice how my thighs pucker into dimples when I sit. I have seen the face she makes. Like it hurts her eyes. Like she is looking at a mirror that reflects what her own legs used to be.

"Are you sure that skirt isn't too short?" she says whenever I try to dress like the Girls. "Maybe you should wear those cute pants I bought you instead."

Every morning before school it's the same: her eyes roam my body, she makes her worried face, and then she suggests I change.

"But everyone wears skirts like this," I tell her.

Worried face.

"But the pants look so nice on you, honey."

Change, her face pleads.

"They're much more . . . flattering."

Please.

She knows. She was a fat girl once, too.

My feet are already sweaty in my new white socks with the red pompoms on the heels. Grace said they were *retro* when one of the girls complained. But Grace is in charge. So everyone believed her and acted like the socks they had worried about one minute ago were now the coolest thing on the planet. *Retro. Yeah.* They all nodded and admired their feet.

A sweater-soft shoulder presses against mine. An unmistakable watermelon scent wafts around me. Paul Mitchell hair spray.

"Hey, Lace," Sammy says, adjusting her skirt. "Thanks for saving me a seat."

Grace and Ben walk past us. They always sit in the seat farthest back. Grace smiles at me, but Ben pretends I don't exist. I'm sure my joining the squad is the very worst thing that has happened to him. Ever.

My brother is not the kind of brother who loves and adores and protects his little sister. My brother wishes I didn't exist. The feeling is mostly mutual.

"Where's Claire?" I ask.

Sammy sighs. "I heard she went home sick."

Heard. It seems strange that she didn't get a message from Claire.

"She thinks she's too good for us," Grace had said this morning in a dismissive way. And that was what Claire was, I guess. Dismissed.

"I like your hair," I tell Sammy. She always waits to pull her hair back until the last minute. She seems to know she looks best with it down. Long and wavy and perfect.

"Yours too!" She smiles and touches my braid.

"Are you excited for the game?" she asks. Sammy is always so perky.

I smile and nod.

"I'm glad you're on the team, Lace. Everyone is. We really needed"—she pauses, and I see her realize that what she was about to say would come out wrong—"you," she finishes.

Me.

I know what that means without the missing phrase before it. What they need is *someone like me.* And what that means is someone my size. Every cheerleading squad needs a few girls *like me.* Strong girls. Big girls. Girls who can hold the others up.

Sammy's expertly curled hair whips my face when she twists around to slap Jacob for making a kissing sound in her ear from behind. I squirm.

He gets up and pushes his way into our seat and practically sits on our laps. This seat is not meant for three.

I slide closer to the side of the bus, pressing my shoulder against the cold metal.

Sammy angles her knees into the aisle like they are a swinging door. Jacob wedges himself between us even more tightly. He makes a point to push his muscular arm against my soft one. Hard.

He is carrying a basketball, as if he needs it to define who he is. A player. A jock. An asshole?

Or just a message: *I'm the star.*

Like we all don't know that already. Like his stupid letter jacket with all the pins and patches doesn't spell it out. MVP. *Most Valuable Player.* I like *Most Vile Prick* better.

This doesn't make me sound like a very good cheerleader. But I'm not here for the boys. I'm here because the Girls asked me to be. Me. No one ever picks me for teams. No one ever picks me for anything. They just pick *on* me.

My ex–best friend, Stephen, said the Girls are only friends with me because of Ben. He said Grace was desperate to save their relationship and she could keep better tabs on him if she had me to help.

She's just using you, Lace. Why else would she want to be friends with you?

Sometimes I think if he hadn't said that, we would still be friends.

Even though he apologized, I know he meant it. How can you stay friends with someone who would say something so mean, even if he was just being honest?

But then there's the other matter. The *other* matter. Of Stephen and Ben. And I'm not sure what to think about that.

ı | | ı ı

Jacob strums the ball with one hand as if he's playing an instrument. The hollow sound makes me feel empty. Like he is tapping *me,* and there is nothing inside.

With his other hand, he reaches for Sammy's perfect pink knee and taps that too. She flashes her polished-white teeth at him. His hand slides farther up her thigh.

He is chewing Trident gum. The blue package flavor. It's my mom's favorite. There is no other reason I would recognize his breath. It makes me feel sick.

He looks at me once. Just once. His eyes travel from my face, down my chest to my lap, and my legs. I try to raise my knees up to make my legs look skinnier and erase the dimples, but he's already done looking. Being disgusted.

Tap-tap tappity-tap.

Hollow. Empty.

Sometimes I think my mother was right. This skirt. This sweater. This outfit. Is not the right costume for me.

But the Girls told me that I would "be great." And that they could "really use me." And that they "needed a strong girl" to help with formations.

"You're the foundation," Grace told me. "You have the most important job of *all.*"

I believed her.

At practice, I let the size zeros climb up me. Tiny feet

on my thighs leaving red imprints. I brace my elbows and place my hands out flat for another step, up to my shoulders.

I am a human jungle gym. A stepladder. Every day.

But I am part of a squad, too. And that's what I like. I like having the same "costume" as everyone else. I like hearing my voice, mostly in unison with all the other girls. I like that Claire always whispers *sorry* as she climbs up me, as if she senses the humiliation I might feel.

The Girls are nice to me. I know I make them look even better than they already do. Stand next to me and you will feel like a supermodel. My presence makes everyone feel better about themselves.

It's not that I'm obese. Just chunky. When I was younger, my mother called my folds "baby fat" and said as long as I ate healthy, I would outgrow it. But I think she was just trying to convince herself. After all, she never outgrew hers.

When the Girls saw me staring at the cheerleading tryouts flyer, they told me I should try out. Grace actually hopped up and down.

"You'd be a great addition to the squad!" Sammy agreed. Sammy is my favorite.

I felt my cheeks get hot. I shook my head and laughed.

"Why is that so funny?" Grace asked.

244

At first I thought she was offended. "Me?" I asked. "A cheerleader?"

"Why not?" She seemed to genuinely want to know.

"Look at me," I said.

She shrugged. "You're beautiful!"

I looked down at my stomach. "And fat."

"Don't say that," Claire said.

"Besides, we need all body types," Grace added.

"Yeah," Sammy said. "You should come to try-outs. We're not like TV cheerleaders. We're nice."

We're nice.

It seemed like a promise.

"It's a big commitment, though," Grace said. "Joining the squad is like joining a second family. We practice every day after school. We spend a *lot* of time together."

She made this sound like it could be a good thing or a bad thing. But to me, it sounded all good. Time away from my mom. Time with my new friends. Time with *nice* people. *Family.*

"I'll do it," I said.

"They'll destroy you," Stephen told me.

But I didn't listen.

"A real friend would be supportive," I said.

"A real friend tells the truth," he replied. "Because I care about you."

245

"You care more about Ben," I said. "Even though you know he treats me like dirt."

I was a real friend telling the truth too.

But neither of us wanted to hear it.

Jacob shifts on the seat so his body angles away from me. His last name crawls across his back in fuzzy letters: *Richarde.* French for Dick.

Someone snickers behind us.

"Do it."

"Do it, man!"

A car honks its horn. I turn to see a line of middle fingers sticking out the row of windows behind us. They look like a formation of angry soldiers. I check to see if Ben is part of this stupidity, but he's just staring miserably out the window. Grace sits next to him, also looking miserable. I've tried, but I just don't understand what it is about Ben that Grace is so in love with. I know he's my brother, but he treats her like crap. Not to mention the other thing I know about him.

The brakes on the bus screech at the next traffic light.

"Hey!" the bus driver yells. "The next finger I see is mine!"

More snickering.

"She wishes," Jacob mutters.

"I'll give her my finger," someone toward the back says suggestively.

Sammy laughs uncomfortably. "Gross."

Jacob's fingers walk higher up her thigh. "What about you?" he whispers at her, loud enough so I'll hear, too.

She looks confused. "What?"

I turn away. Press myself harder against the cold metal. I do not want to be part of this conversation. I do not want to be in this seat. But Jacob elbows me, as if he wants me to pay attention.

He presses his middle finger into Sammy's thigh and makes a swirling motion, then moves the finger as if it's a person walking up her thigh. It peeks under the hem of her skirt.

"Stop it." Sammy pushes his hand back down toward her knee. But the finger person comes back. It hesitates at the hem. Waits. For permission?

Sammy shoves his hand away again. He whispers something in her ear I can't hear.

I study the back of the seat in front of me. There are six different-size pieces of petrified gum stuck to it. Two pinkish-gray. One brownish-red. One light green. One bright purple. One baby blue. I guess the flavors. Strawberry. Cinnamon. Spearmint, obviously. Grape, also obvious. Winter mint.

Each one is squished flat. You could probably see the person's fingerprint on them. I wonder if they were all put there by the same person. A kid? A boy? A girl? I wonder what the person was thinking as he or she pushed the gum onto its final resting place. I'm going to guess it was a girl. A mad girl. Or a sad girl. Who likes gum.

Why can't she just put it back in the wrapper and throw it away later? Because she doesn't want to make the effort. Because she doesn't care. Or maybe she is trying to be the "bad girl." Maybe she is trying to make a statement. It's probably not the best one. Right now, the statement is telling me this girl doesn't have a gum preference and she doesn't mind staring at her own disgusting petrified chewed-up gum day after day. And she doesn't care that the rest of us have to look at it. And she isn't worried about brushing her backpack or sleeve against the gum when she stands up. So that must mean . . .

She doesn't care about herself. And maybe no one else does, either.

Maybe she feels like a chewed-up, spit-out piece of gum herself.

I feel sorry for this girl I don't know. If I knew who she was, I would try to be her friend.

ı | | ı ı

"I said stop it!" Sammy says louder than before.

Jacob is trying again to reach up Sammy's skirt. I don't want to see, but the movement from the corner of my eye distracts me.

Jacob sighs in an exasperated way.

I don't know why she lets him sit next to her.

Jacob *Richarde.*

The Dick.

I snicker. I can't help it.

"Freak," Jacob whispers at me before he gets up and moves back to the seat behind us.

Sammy sits quietly and stares at the gum.

I wonder if she feels chewed up now, too.

II.

The away team's school gym is smaller than ours. The bleachers are creaky. Jacob sits down and rocks back and forth, making a rude gesture that is supposed to be him having sex with the air. The rest of the boys crack up as expected, even Ben. The cheerleaders roll their eyes. I just stare. When Jacob notices me, he widens his eyes and rocks toward me, like I'm the one he wants to have sex with. Only, I know he doesn't, so I look away while all the boys laugh even harder. I don't check to see if Ken does.

The coach walks over and tells the boys to suit up in the locker room. I am glad to see them go.

Across the gym floor, the other team's fans shake cowbells at us like an angry mob. They stomp their feet to the song playing through speakers on the ceiling.

"We Will Rock You," by Queen.

It's such a weird way of saying, *We are going to win.*

I bet that's not even what the song is about.

Grace gathers us into a huddle. "Remember to smile," she tells us. "And enunciate your words." She says this last very slowly, stressing each syllable and moving her mouth in an exaggerated way. Like her lips have a life of their own. Then she hands us each a lemon drop. I don't even know why. Something to do with *e-nun-ci-a-tion?* I unwrap the clear plastic and put the drop in my mouth. The outside is sweet and sugary but then turns sour. The other girls make faces as they reach their own sour middles. But no one complains. We just keep sucking.

Even though all I taste is sour, in this moment, being part of this circle with our arms tight around one another's shoulders, I feel the sweetness of being part of something.

"Where's Claire?" one of the girls asks.

"She went home sick from school," Grace explains. "So, Megan, you'll take her position."

Sammy makes a sad face. I can tell she misses her.

I wonder if Claire was really sick, or just sick of us. The way we ignored her this morning, I wouldn't blame her.

When it's time to introduce the teams, we follow Grace in a perfectly formed line with our hands on our hips and our red-and-white pompoms shaking at our sides. Each step is a double swish.

Swish-swish.

Swish-swish.

If anyone goes out of step, the rhythm will break. I concentrate on my swishing and try to ignore the way my thigh fat jiggles to the whisper-beat of the pompoms.

Jiggle-swish.

Jiggle-swish.

When we get to the corner of the gym where our team will make their grand appearance, we form two lines facing each other. We raise our pompoms in the air and join them with the girls across from us to make a red-and-white tunnel ceiling for the boys to run through. My bridge partner is usually Claire, so now I get the skinniest of the skinny girls, Megan. She is chewing gum, which is against the rules. For a brief moment I imagine she is my

Gum Girl. I imagine she is more than what Stephen used to say about the cheerleaders and especially the Girls. That they're empty. She smiles at me and I smile back. We press our pompoms together, sealing the tunnel roof.

The announcer calls each player's name and position, and the boys come running out one at a time like superstars. Their sneakers squeak on the gleaming floor. Their pristine basketballs *bounce-bounce-bounce* as they dribble past. They have to hunch down to get through our too-low pompom-covered tunnel. Once through, they dribble up to the basket and do a layup.

Swish.

Each one high-fives the one who followed. Like it is such a big deal to make a basket. Like they are *Such. Big. Deals.*

No one else but the cheerleaders applaud. It's rough, playing at the other team's school, surrounded by people who want to see you lose.

When the home team comes out, the crowd goes wild. The cowbells shake in a more supportive way. The foghorns blow. The foot stomps are deafening. Our boys and the cheerleaders stand respectfully. Clap politely. But I can see on their faces that they are imagining how our team will take the home team down. It is not an attractive look.

After the teams warm up at opposite ends of the gym, the home-team cheerleaders perform a routine on the floor. One boy goes out with them. He is not a mascot but a real cheerleader. He is wearing the same sweater-vest as the girls, but instead of a skirt, he has shorts. Our boys snicker. Cough out the familiar words they use for anyone not on their "team."

Homo.

Fag.

Queer.

Ben does it the loudest.

I think of Stephen and wish he was here. If he saw this side of Ben, maybe he wouldn't be so stupid about him. Maybe he would realize that Ben doesn't deserve him.

Thinking of Stephen makes my chest hurt. The space he used to occupy there is cold and empty and starving.

He says I'm the one who ruined our friendship by choosing the Girls over him. But I say *he* is the one who ruined our friendship by choosing Ben.

What is it about Ben that makes people so crazy? I will never understand. If Stephen could hear Ben now, hear him say those words with disgust in his throat . . . Well, I guess I'm glad he can't. No one deserves to be hurt like that.

"Knock it off, boys," the coach says in a playful way.

I can tell he wants to wink at them. Cough those words with them. He makes me want to puke.

I wonder if the cheerboy can hear them. If he knows what they're saying. I wonder if it feels the same way when I hear the familiar words they use for people like me.

Thunder thighs.

Wide load.

Porker.

Chubber.

Pudge muffin.

I wish the cheerboy would look at me. I would like to silently tell him, *You are brave. You are a hero.* Even though he is not a very good cheerleader.

When they finish their performance, we cheerleaders stand up and clap that way snooty women do, tapping our fingers into our palms to achieve the look of approval but not the sound.

Then we stand and follow Grace out on the floor to perform our own routine.

"Ready, girls?"

"Hit it!"

My thighs bounce and ripple with every jump. Stomp. Pivot. My too-big breasts flop wildly despite the expensive sports bra I saved up for that promised—*promised*—this would not happen.

I wait for the laughter from the boys on the bench. The strangers from the home team. They will not cough their insults. They will *enunciate* them.

Earthquake!

When we turn to face the home side, I search out the cheerboy. I don't know why he became my instant hero. Because he stands out like me? He seems like my kindred spirit. Like we should be friends. Like Stephen used to be.

But when I spot him, he is sitting in the front row, in the middle of the line of cheerleaders. They surround him protectively. He is laughing. Pointing.

At me.

My heart skips and then it dies a little. I feel it shrink. The empty space for Stephen widens. It is a chasm.

But the show must go on. The show. Starring the magnificent fat girl with the incredible bouncing boobs.

I plant my feet on the shiny wood floor. Bend my knees, also known as soft stepping-stones, for Megan to use as she climbs up me. The stepladder.

She presses her slender foot onto my cushion thigh— the first rung—then my shoulder, as we slowly create our BIG! FORMATION!

Go, team!

Megan's crisp white sneakers dig into my already-bruised shoulders. If you inspect the purple mark carefully, you will see the dainty outline of her footprint. But I SMILE! Then Sammy begins the climb, and I am holding the weight of one and a half. The other ladder girls next to me grin the way I do. They aren't as chubby as me, but they are "big-boned," as my mother would say. "Strong girls," as Grace would say. I'm sure they are thinking, like I am, that it would be nice to be the climber and not the climbed on for once.

We chant, "Who's gonna win? Ir-ving!"

My legs shake under Sammy's weight, even though she probably weighs less than one hundred pounds and most likely had celery for lunch because, as she always reminds us, it is the perfect food. You burn the amount of calories it has just by chewing it.

Yum.

The first time I brought my own celery sticks out during practice, some of the girls gasped. They were filled with peanut butter and a line of raisins.

"Oh! I used to love ants on a log." Sammy had said. "I miss peanut butter."

"Do you want a bite?" I asked.

"Can't," she said, patting her flat—almost concave, I swear—tummy. "I'm on a diet."

Oh.

ı | | ı ı

When we finish our formation, I count silently to ten. That's how long we have to hold it to truly impress. Sammy is somewhere high above me. Sammy the smallest. The cutest. The loudest.

The boys from our team are all watching Sammy. Probably they are trying to see up her skirt.

Jacob makes another rude gesture with his finger.

Then the girls jump down, and we all jog off the court, elbows bent at ninety-degree angles, hands in pompoms at the base of our backs like they are bustles on a dress. *Shake-shake-shake.* I feel like a show pony. Or no. A circus elephant.

We have to jog right by our boys' team, who sit in the front row of the bleachers with their long legs sticking out. They make whistles and rude comments as we jog past. I pretend not to hear and focus on the *swish-swish-swish* of my pompoms on my back. All the way to the safety of my spot at the end of the bench to watch the game. To cheer the boys on, even though they are so awful to us. We're not here for them, though. We're here for *us.*

Go, team!

Or whatever.

III.

Even though our boys have nicer uniforms and our school is bigger and our coach probably makes more money than the other team's, we lose. I think it was the cowbells and the horns and the constant foot stomping. It is hard to perform under such negative circumstances. It was Jacob who nearly saved the day. Not Ben, the usual hero. Jacob was "on fire" tonight, according to the coach. And I suppose he was pretty good. Sometimes, people transform when they are doing what they love. On the court, Jacob is grace. He weaves through the players, the ball an extension of his body that he releases, but that comes back to him, like they are meant to be together. Jacob *Richarde* may be a dick, but when he is playing basketball, I will admit, he is beautiful. Even the other team cheered for him when he made an impossible shot in the last quarter. But it was Sammy who led us in a cheer just for him. Who seemed to forget the not-beautiful off-the-court Jacob and hugged his sweaty body after the game when the boys walked over to the stands, defeated.

No one is in a good mood as we find our way to the bus through the cold, dark parking lot. I find a different seat and hope I will get lucky and no one will sit with me.

Rides home in the dark are for hooking up. And that is not for me.

The bus in dark. I just want to lean my head against the cold glass window despite the dirty handprint smudges I know are there. Out of sight but not really out of my mind. How I would like to be.

But just as the bus begins to heave itself forward, someone slides in next to me and presses tight against my side so that it is hard to breathe. The smell of his blue Trident gum gives him away. He doesn't have his basket-ball. Or Sammy.

I scan the dark bus to try to find her, but I can't see. I want to tell him he has the wrong seat. But he whispers, "Hey, Lacy," and presses harder against me.

I close my eyes and press the side of my face against the glass. Maybe if I don't talk to him, he will go away.

Hot fingers squeeze my leg. He has me pressed so tightly against the side of the bus that my arms are trapped at my sides. I tighten the muscles on my thigh. Shake it, to loosen his grasp. But he squeezes harder. I smell his blue Trident gum breath again. His face is so close I can hear the *snap-snap* of him chewing.

"Lacy, you are oddly hot," he whispers. He pushes his nose into the nape of my neck and sniffs. "Yeah. You could be beautiful if you dropped a few pounds."

Here is when I am supposed to scream.

Here is when I am supposed to push back.

But I am trapped silent and still, and I don't know why.

I wiggle one hand free and try to push him away. But he is strong and his fingers slide under my skirt. One finger wedges between my squeezed-together thighs. The nail scrapes my skin like a sharp-toothed worm. It pokes, pokes, and finds my panties.

I want to cry out. I want to scream. I want to kick and flail.

But I am so alone on this dark bus. Where everyone hooks up on the ride home. Even me.

Poke.

I choke and jerk my body to make him stop.

I dig my fingers into his arm, but they don't claw him because I have bitten the nails to the nub.

Warm tears slip quietly down my cheeks.

"Lacy," he whispers.

Poke.

I squirm again. Squeeze my legs tighter. Smell blue Trident. Feel like I am the one being chewed up now.

"C'mon, Lacy. You know you want it. I saw you watching me on the court."

But that is a lie. The Jacob on the court is not this

Jacob. And if I know anything, it is that I do not want *it*. I do not want his finger touching me. Hurting me. That is what I know.

And finally. Finally. I find my voice.

"STOP IT!"

The sound is a scream I never knew was inside me.

The bus goes quiet.

He pulls his hand back. Laughs awkwardly. I feel his anger next to me.

Dark silhouetted heads turn our way. Faceless without the light. Still, I can feel their anticipation. Something big just happened. Something they will be texting about later. And whisper-talking about at school.

What are Sammy and Grace thinking?

What is Ben?

What would Claire think if she was here? What would Stephen?

Would *anyone* stand up for me?

Silence. Waiting.

I feel it. I'm sure Jacob can too. It is the make-or-break moment for both of us. I cower in my seat and press myself back against it as hard as I can.

Jacob lifts his middle finger to the crowd and wiggles it.

"Who else wants it?" he asks.

In the dark, his finger looks like a black snake. Dirty. And sickening.

More tears stream down my cheeks. Catch on my jaw. Drip off into nothing. Or maybe onto him.

The person in the seat in front of us leans closer toward us. It's Sammy.

She looks at the finger. Then at me.

Her mouth drops open. Anger. There is anger. The shadows on her face are sharp. Her features even more pointed.

"What the hell?" she asks.

But I don't know if she's talking to me or him.

I am trapped. Trapped again. My voice lost again at the shock of what just happened. At what a person is capable of. And what I am not.

Shame travels through me. Hot. Dark. Like poison.

I sink into the seat and cross my legs. I don't care about the cottage cheese. It's too dark to see anyway. I pull my skirt over my scratched and stinging thighs. The fabric, so soft, feels grossly comforting.

Jacob moves away from me. Gets up and slides in next to Sammy.

"Don't even think about it," she says.

But he just laughs. A bunch of boys whistle.

Where is Ben?

Where is my brother, who is supposed to stand up for me?

But I know. He's pretending as usual. That he's not my brother. That he's just a dumb jock. That he's in love with Grace and not . . .

Stephen.

Stephen was right. I should never have listened to the Girls. I should never have become a cheerleader.

Jacob's head moves closer to Sammy's. Now he is smelling the nape of *her* neck.

She whispers, "Stop it. Stop it."

And he slithers away into the dark.

I throw up in my mouth.

The bus gets quiet again. We bump along through the night.

I hug my arms over my fuzzy sweater. My *I*. For *Irving.*

For *I am all alone.*

And all I can think is my mother was right.

This costume doesn't suit me at all.

IV.

In the parking lot back at school, Sammy grabs my shoulders. "Are you OK?" she asks.

I don't know how to answer.

"I'll handle this," she says. She hugs me, but then runs after Jacob and gets in his car, and they drive away.

Those of us who don't drive yet wait under the parking lot lights for our rides.

Grace and Ben go off in Grace's car.

Neither of them look happy.

Megan comes to stand next to me. "Do you need a ride?" she asks softly. "I'm sure my mom could give you one."

Maybe she will be my new friend. Or does she just want to be one of the Girls?

"Thanks," I say. I text my parents to tell them Ben and I don't need rides.

As we stand there, I notice Megan isn't chewing gum anymore. I wonder if there is a new piece on the back of that seat on the bus.

She smiles sadly at me and looks away. Me, away. Me, away. Over and over. Finally, she reaches over and takes my hand.

"Are you all right?" she asks. "Jacob is so disgusting. I don't see what Sammy likes about him."

Her hand feels warm and sure in mine. But small. And weak. And temporary. And foreign.

I don't answer.

The bus pulls away and goes wherever buses go when they are done for the day. I watch it disappear into the night and know I will never get on it again.

At home, I tell my parents I'm tired and don't feel like eating the food they left out for me and Ben. My mom never objects to me skipping a meal. "No worries," she says happily. "I'm sure Ben will gladly eat your share." My dad looks worried but doesn't speak up. He never contradicts my mom.

"Ben got a ride with Grace," I tell them.

My mom and dad exchange relieved smiles.

"They are such a cute couple," my mother says.

"She seems like a nice girl," my dad agrees.

I go to my room and shut the door.

I undress in the dark. I fold my costume neatly. I put on my baggy pajama pants and my T-shirt that comes down to my knees. I sit on my bed and wait for my parents to go to their room, where they'll watch TV in bed. I wait to hear the familiar sound of the lady from *House Hunters* coming down the hall.

Quietly I pick up my costume and walk down the hallway to the kitchen. I open the trash compactor and lift out the evening's trash. Two Lean Cuisine containers. An empty bag of spinach. Crumpled paper napkins. I hold my breath as I lift things out, then slowly place my costume inside. I cover it up carefully with the Lean Cuisine containers. The plastic spinach bag. The napkins. I rip off some paper towel pieces from the roll on the counter and put those on top, just to make sure the red and white don't show.

Then I slide it closed and press Compact.

I listen as the machine does its magic, squishing the insides down, down, down into a small flat box. Squishing my costume flat as a skinny pancake. Flat as a chewed-up piece of gum on the sidewalk that's been stepped on a thousand times. Into nothing.

I stare at the red dot on the button and listen to the quiet motor inside, pressing, pressing, pressing.

That costume wasn't right for me. It isn't me.

So why can't I breathe?

Why . . .

Can't I breathe?

I press the button again and wait for the light to turn green.

I fish out the stained paper towels. The flattened spinach bag. The Lean Cuisine packaging. The napkins. And then my costume. I leave the trash on the counter, the compactor drawer open, and go back to my room.

I pull off my baggy sweatpants and T-shirt and put my costume back on. No, not my costume. My uniform.

It is wrinkled but not ruined. Stained but not a lost cause.

I take a deep breath.

Let it out.

Deep breath.

Let it out.

In my mirror, I stare at the girl Sammy said is beautiful.

I step closer to her.

I turn one way, then the other. I plant my feet as if I am going to hold up my teammates.

We need strong girls like you.

I smile the way Grace taught me.

For a moment, I see a glimpse of beauty in mirror me. A glimpse of strength.

When I step back, my thighs rub together and sting where Jacob hurt me. Tried. Tried to hurt me.

I spread my feet apart so my thighs don't touch. I make the Λ position, hands on hips.

Ready, girl?

Hit it.

I stretch my arms to the ceiling in a *V* for victory.

Mirror me mouths, *Go, team!*

And I whisper back, *Go, me!*

Then, I find my phone in my backpack and text Stephen.

I miss you, I type.

Can we talk?

NINE:
STAY GOLD
(Grace: 8:05 p.m.)

I.

BEN'S HAND IN MIND IS LIKE A CLAMMY, DEAD eel. I squeeze it, and it doesn't squeeze back. I look at him, and he doesn't look back. I love him, and he doesn't love back.

We used to be an *us*. A *we*. One. But the secret, his secret, cut us back in two.

The bus is crowded and loud. There's a mixture of strong cologne, perfume, and sweat in the air. I used to like this smell. It made me feel alive and excited. It's the smell of the after-game rush. Ben and I used to sit in this seat, riding home from a great game and performance, and I would feel like we were king and queen. Like we were on top of it all. Now I feel like we're being squished under *it all's* weight

I let go of his hand and smooth my skirt over my thighs. No one talks to us. No one cares. We lost the game and everyone thinks it's Ben's fault, and that means it's my fault too. Isn't it my job to make him happy? To cheer him up? To be his number-one fan?

I'm glad it's dark so no one can see that I'm crying. I don't want anyone to see the mascara running down my cheeks, giving me a sad-clown face.

Everything has turned out to be pretend. Even my expression.

This morning my little sister, Beth, told me that I didn't look right. She said my armor was tarnished. When I asked her what she meant, she shrugged and stuffed her face with a chocolate Pop-Tart.

"Do you know how many calories those have?" I asked. Sometimes I can't help myself.

"Who cares?" she asked through a mouthful. Her teeth were covered with wet brown crumbs, making them look rotten.

"Gross," I said.

She chugged down a glass of milk and smiled. Her teeth were still coated.

"I think you're bossy because you're sad and it makes you feel empowered to tell people what to do."

"Thanks, Dear Abby," I said. "But I don't remember asking for advice." Beth is eleven and reads advice columns for fun. She's always quoting her words of wisdom at me. My parents think it's cute. They think everything Beth does is brilliant and quirky and special, and everything I do is cold and calculated and unoriginal. Having a cheerleader for a daughter seems to be their ultimate shame.

Actually I don't know if that's true. But that's how they make me feel. "Surprise us, Grace!" they're always saying. "Stop being so *predictable*."

Beth is always telling me I'm like a cutout from a teen romance novel. Head cheerleader. Blond. Perfect body. Hot jock boyfriend who is captain of the basketball team. Popular. Smart. She tells me there has to be something more to me than the stereotype I try to emulate, but I don't let anyone see what the "more thing" is. I hate that she uses words like *emulate*.

I never *tried* to create my image. It's just who I am. I *like* being head cheerleader. I *like* being fit. I *like* my silky hair. I *like* having the cutest boyfriend in school.

What's so wrong with that?

Only, I'm about to lose that last one. I bet my family will be ecstatic.

When I left Beth in the kitchen this morning, she was opening another silver Pop-Tart packet. "Have a good day!" she yelled. "I'm sorry you're feeling sad!"

"I'm not sad!" I yelled back.

But we both knew it was a lie.

I squeeze Ben's eel hand again. Nothing. Maybe what's wrong with wanting to be perfect is that there's no such thing.

Out of nowhere, someone screams.

I squint in the dark and see Jacob doing something with his middle finger. I can't see what's going on.

"I think that was Lacy," I say to Ben.

"Oh, God," he mutters.

"Do you think she's OK?" I whisper.

"She's just a freak," he says.

I cringe. Before Lacy and I became friends, I might have laughed and agreed, even though she's his sister. Now I want to punch him. I take my hand out of his and wipe the cold sweat from it on my skirt.

"She's nice," I say.

"Whatever."

"What is *wrong* with you?" I ask.

"Nothing." He leans his head against the window.

I lean my head against the back of the seat. I try to remember what it was about Ben that I thought I loved so much. Has he always been such a jerk and I'm just seeing it now?

No.

No, I know he was different before. He was sweet and funny. And *hot* and *sexy* and definitely the best-looking guy our school has ever seen. He was . . . perfect.

What's wrong with that?

Oh, yeah.

Beth calls him Ken. As in Barbie's boyfriend. The first time she said it, my parents laughed so hard that my dad started coughing and my mom had to pound him on the back to make him stop, and wine came out his nose and at first we all thought he'd given himself a nosebleed. I secretly wished he had.

"You're all so mean!" I yelled.

"Oh, Grace, relax," my mom said.

She's always telling me to relax. "You're so serious. So motivated. You need to learn how to chill out, honey. You're going to give yourself ulcers."

When my mother tells me stuff like this, it's hard not to hate her. What kind of parent doesn't want their daughter to be popular and get good grades and be head of the cheerleading squad and have a cute boyfriend? I swear, I think they'd be happier if I was a stoner or something like they were when *they* were in high school. God.

Sometimes I wonder if I've stayed with Ben as long as I have just to annoy my family. There aren't a whole lot of other good reasons at the moment. Especially now that I know that . . .

Now that I know . . .

That it's over.

If my parents found out the truth about Ben, they would probably both die laughing. They would find the whole story so funny and tell it to all their friends. I think that's the worst thing of all. Knowing for sure that this is what they would do. They wouldn't be sad for me. They wouldn't see that I'm hurt. They would just think how hysterical it is that the boy I picked just because he's supposed to be Mr. Perfect turned out to . . .

Like boys.

I look at Ben, not looking at me, probably daydreaming about *him*. Stephen.

He can deny it but I know. I saw.

I know! I saw!

I'm not perfect. I'm so far from perfect that my boyfriend prefers being with a boy to being with me.

I can't help it, he said when he finally admitted it. *I'm sorry. I don't know what's wrong with me.*

Tears. More tears. Panic. And me, holding him like he was a baby.

Hating him and loving him at the same time.

Comforting him and wanting to hurt him.

I reach over for his hand again. He finally squeezes mine like we used to. I squeeze back. *I love you.* But I know it's hopeless.

II.

The bus pulls into the parking lot. Because we're in the last seat, we have to wait for everyone to get off before us. A few guys turn back to tell Ben, "Good job tonight," but we all know it isn't true. He lost the game for us. Even the coach said so. "Why are you so distracted, Mead? Get your head in the game!"

But he fouled out in the third quarter and sat with his head in his hands the rest of the game. We cheerleaders kept up our cheers and claps and yells, but without Ben the team was doomed. Even Jacob, the second-best player, couldn't carry the team without him.

We sit in the dark and wait. I can feel the disappointment surrounding us. The hopelessness as everyone slowly shuffles down the narrow aisle. Finally, I stand up and Ben follows me. We step outside into the cold, and without me asking, he follows me to my car. I know he doesn't want to do this. I know it's all just pretend. He wants the guys to see him get in the car with me so they'll think we're still a couple.

I wave good night to Lacy. A good friend would offer to drive her home. That's probably what she's thinking. And more. She must know about Ben. She must. But she's never said anything to me. Never hinted, while we drove for hours looking for her brother, that my search was in vain. Even if I found Ben, I would never find the Ben I was looking for.

Just like perfect, he doesn't exist.

Ben and I drive through town without talking. When I signal to turn onto his street, though, he says, "Don't."

He reaches over and touches my hand. "I don't want to go home."

"Don't," I repeat.

"Grace," he says. "I'm sorry. Can we go somewhere to talk? Please?"

I sigh and turn off the signal. "Where?" I ask quietly.

"I don't care."

It's a horrible answer. I decide to drive us back to the high school, winding through side streets. We don't talk. By the time we get back, everyone's gone and the parking lot lights highlight its emptiness.

"Why back here?" he asks.

We both stare at the main entrance to the school.

"I've always loved this school," I say. "I love being a cheerleader. Being popular. Being good at . . . everything. When I'm here, I feel good about myself."

I know what this makes me sound like. Shallow. Stupid. A Barbie. But I'm not any of those things. I'm just Grace. Trying to tell the truth.

"I wish I could be like you," Ben says.

"You could be," I tell him. I know it's probably a lie, but I want to believe it. I know it's not fair, but I want it to be true.

"I hate who I am," he says sadly. "I wish I could be someone else."

"You can be whoever you want to be," I say, as if it's that easy.

He shakes his head and then bangs it hard against the headrest. "You know that's not true."

"Yes, it is," I say. "You just don't want to because you're scared."

He sighs. "I thought you of all people would understand."

"What's that supposed to mean?"

"You're all about image, right? You care what people think about you. You work so hard to be . . . perfect."

"Just like you."

He sighs again. He is perfect at sighing.

"Right. Just like me. Only with me, it's a lie."

"You think you can't be like me if everyone knows your secret?"

"I know I can't."

He's right, of course. I don't want him to be, but he is. I saw the players making fun of the boy cheerleader at the game tonight. I heard the names.

"Can we walk?" Ben asks. "I need air."

We get out and start walking down the sidewalk along the edge of the parking lot. We are just the exact right height together. Him just a few inches taller than me. When we slow-dance, his shoulder is the exact height for me to rest my head on. We walk over to the concrete steps leading up to the doors of the school and sit on the top

278

ones under a light. This is our throne. King and queen of the school.

Or queen and queen, I think. I smile a little. It's something Beth would say, and I'm surprised a Beth-like thought would enter my head. But then I realize it's really not that funny.

With the light shining down, Ben's eyelash shadows reach down his strong cheekbones. I love his dimples. His perfect jawline.

My legs are cold and I squeeze them together. But he takes off his jacket and puts it over my lap like a blanket.

"It's funny," he says, "how alike you and I are."

I reach for his hand out of habit. It's cold.

"Almost perfect," he says.

"Nearly," I agree.

We sit quietly, letting the truth settle in.

"I guess this is where we break up," I say.

He lets go of my hand so that he can put his arm around me.

"I love you," he says. "It's so messed up. I know I love you. But . . . I can't . . ."

"Be with me."

I want to tell him I love him too. But I don't really know if I do anymore. I love his hair. I love his dimples. I love his strong jawline. I love his hand in mine. I love watching him play basketball, and I love sitting here with him, like we are king and queen.

But I don't know if I love *him*.

I rest my head on his shoulder, where it fits so perfectly. So temporarily.

"You cheated on me," I tell him.

"I'm sorry."

"I know."

I feel something wet on my face and wipe it off. A tear.

"I'm so screwed up," he says.

I reach up and erase the wet trail of tears on his cheek with my thumb.

"You can't help it," I say. I know this is true. My uncle is gay and he told me all about what it was like for him, denying it for so long. Now he's married and has two kids. He's happy. His husband, my other uncle, is hot. Kind of like Ben. Everything turned out all right for him.

That's what I hope for Ben. I feel it now. That hope. Deep in my heart. So maybe I love him after all.

"This isn't the end of the world," I tell him.

"Why does it feel like it?"

"My sister would say because you're self-centered." I smile so he knows I don't mean it in a bad way.

He squeezes me tighter. "Your sister is such a little bitch."

"I know. I wish I could be more like her, though."

"I like you just the way you are."

"Too bad I'm not a boy."

He stiffens next to me.

"C'mon," I say. "We can talk about it."

He doesn't say anything.

"I'm not going to tell anyone," I say. "But I won't be your fake girlfriend, either."

"I'm sorry," he says. "I'm sorry I disappointed you."

"You didn't disappoint me. You hurt me."

"I'm sorry for that too."

"What will you do now? Will you keep pretending?"

I stare at his shadow lashes. Blinking away tears again.

"I don't know what to do," he says. "I don't know who I am. I know it sounds so pathetic, but, Grace, I really am confused. I don't want to be like this. I don't want to have feelings for . . . anyone but you. But I can't help it. I don't know what's wrong with me."

"Nothing's wrong with you, Ben. Being gay isn't wrong."

"I'm not gay!"

"Then how do you explain Stephen?"

"I don't know! Maybe it's just Stephen, you know? I don't feel the way I feel about him with anyone else."

"I'm not an expert," I tell him. "Maybe you're bi?"

He sits forward and covers his face with his hands. "I hate this. I hate it! I just want to go back to the way things were."

I'm about to say *me too,* but the more I think about it, the more I know that's not true. I don't think I ever believed Ben was really into me. He was always tentative. Always kind of fake. This is the most I've ever felt him want to touch me at all. Because it's safe now. He knows I don't expect more than a hug and holding hands. He'll never have to force himself to kiss me again.

"I just want to be normal," he says sadly.

"There's no such thing," I answer.

I smooth his jacket over my legs. I touch the fuzzy letter *I.* The pins he's earned for varsity and captain. This is what we care about. How many pins we have. We want to be MVPs. The most valuable of all.

What's so wrong with that?

It's stupid, Beth would say. That's what's wrong with it.

I stand and turn to him. "I should take you home now," I say.

I reach out my hand and he takes it. I pull him up. We stand for a minute, under the light. It flickers and makes a zapping sound, as if it's about to go out. But for now, I imagine it's a spotlight shining down on us. The king and queen's last appearance.

We both seem to be drinking it in, this last time together. Then we step down into the dark.

III.

When I pull into the driveway at Ben's, the light is still on in Lacy's room. I cringe, thinking how I used her to get to Ben. It's all true. But she's a friend *now,* and that's what counts. I hope. I haven't been the greatest friend to anyone since I started dating Ben, come to think of it. Especially poor Claire. God. The boy really has made me a little crazy.

"I guess this is it?" Ben asks.

"Yeah," I say. "I guess so."

He leans over and hugs me, but this time his arms feel awkward and clumsy with the steering wheel in the way.

"Good luck with everything," I say. "You're going to be OK."

He nods. "You too."

It's funny, and this is going to sound annoying, but I never doubted that.

I drive away before he gets to the front door. I can't stand watching him walk away from me one more time.

I turn on the radio and blast the volume as I drive home.

At the traffic light just before my house, I see someone staggering down the middle of the road toward me. When the light turns green, he trips into the intersection and stretches out his arms, beckoning me forward.

I flash my lights at him to signal for him to get out of the way, but instead he starts screaming at me.

"Hit me! Just do it!"

I don't move. It's late and there aren't any cars on the road. I don't know if I should honk my horn. I reach over to my armrest and press the button that locks all the doors. My broken heart races to life.

"Dooooo it!" the guy yells again.

The light turns red. The guy walks closer to my car. I still don't know what to do, so I stay put. I grip the steering wheel more tightly with my shaking hands.

Then the guy's standing right in front of me. He starts pounding on the hood of the car.

"Hit me, goddamn it!"

I press the horn and he jumps back, then laughs. He's either drunk or insane.

I inch the car forward a foot. He runs toward me and slams his fists against the front of the car again. I honk several times.

"Bitch!" he yells.

He gives me the finger and laughs.

What the hell? I feel a jolt of anger mix with the adrenaline already coursing through me. I roll my window down just a crack.

"Hey!" I yell. No one calls me a bitch, and definitely no one gives *me* the finger. "Get out of the way!"

I realize this is incredibly stupid behavior on my part. My heart is pounding in a way it never has. It makes me feel alive in some new way I can't name. I should be terrified, but instead I suddenly feel . . . powerful. Like my heart is pumping some kind of new wild energy through my body.

"Make me!" he slurs.

Oh, please. "I have had a crappy day!" I yell. "So you better move it!"

"Yeah, well, I've had a crappy *life*! So whuddayou think about *that*?"

"That's not *my* fault!"

He walks over to my window. I think we recognize

each other at the same time. It's Mr. French, the janitor from school.

"You," he says, staggering back.

Oh my God. I just got in a fight with the janitor?

"Mr. French?" I ask. "Are you OK?" He's always so nice at school, I can't believe he's the same guy.

"You!" he yells again. "Little Miss Perfect."

I don't believe this.

"What so wrong with being perfect?" I call through my window. All this time, I thought he liked me.

Now that he's not in front of the car, I can easily pull through the light and get away. But the light turned red again. Figures. Little Miss Perfect does not run the light.

"Think you're better than everyone!" he slurs.

"No, I don't," I say.

He presses his hands against my window. One of them is bleeding.

"Are you all right?" I ask again.

"Whuddayoucare?"

"You're bleeding."

"So what?"

"Do you want me to call nine-one-one?"

He waves his hand at me. "Who cares? No one."

"I care," I say. "What happened to you?"

He puts his face up to the crack. "Everything. Everything happened to me, OK?"

The light turns green.

"I'm sorry," I say. "I have to go."

I inch forward, hoping he'll step away, but he runs in front of the car again.

"Please move," I say. "Or let me call for help."

"Just listen," he says. "Just listen to me."

"OK."

"I'm sorry," he says.

"It's OK," I tell him.

"No, it's not. I . . . I . . . I can't. I did something."

"You're hurt," I say.

"No. I hit this deer. A long time ago. And then today I . . ."

Blue lights flash behind us. It's a police car. Mr. French swears and runs away, into the dark. One police officer jumps out of the car and takes off after him. I have no idea what I'm supposed to do, so I pull through the intersection and next to the curb. The cruiser follows me and the driver gets out. I feel like I'm going to throw up.

The cop shines a flashlight into my car as he approaches. I roll down the window.

"Sorry," I say. "That guy kept jumping in front of the car when I tried to go through the light."

He shines his flashlight in my face, then down my body. "Cheerleader?" he asks

I nod. What does he think, I was at a costume party?

"I'm driving home from our game," I say.

"You win?"

"No."

"You know that guy?"

I'm about to say yes, but then I just . . . don't. I know Mr. French is usually really nice. And he seemed so upset. "No," I lie. "Just some crazy guy, I guess."

"You shouldn't drive alone at night."

"I live really close."

"That obviously doesn't mean anything."

"I guess."

"Did that guy do anything to you?"

"No. Just . . . got blood on the window. I think he's suicidal. I—I'm worried about him."

"You sure you don't know him?"

"Not really," I say. "No."

He looks at me funny. "Well, you better get home. I'll follow to see you get there safely."

"You don't have to do that."

"But I'm going to."

He walks back to his cruiser and says something on his radio. Slowly, I pull back onto the road and creep along all the way home, terrified to go over the speed limit. As soon as I pull into our driveway and open the garage door, I feel an overwhelming sense of relief and dread. I press the garage remote and close the door, leaving the cop to drive away.

I sit and wait for my heart to stop racing before getting out of the car and going inside. Even when I calm down, my heart still doesn't feel right. It feels like it's been punched around and now it is bruised and aching. And tired. Can a heart feel tired? I don't know. Maybe it's just worn out.

IV.

Inside, the house is quiet and warm. My parents are in the living room staring at their laptops and drinking wine. I say hi but don't stop to chat. They don't ask me about the game or who won. They never do.

I walk slowly down the hall and stop at Beth's door. There's a giant sign on it. She always makes signs for her door. Little messages or warnings for me. Passive-aggressive notes for me to digest. My parents love the cleverness of it all. My door is blank. I don't like clutter. I don't like posters. I don't like messages. I don't need them.

I stand outside the door and read Beth's latest note for me. The paper is blue and the lettering is bright yellow. There are stars all around the message, which reads: "STAY GOLD."

I don't know what it means. But it seems like the most positive thing she's ever left for me. Stay gold. Stay. She thinks I'm gold? What does that even mean?

I tap on her door.

"Who *is* it?" she sings, knowing full well.

"Me," I say.

I hear her jump off her bed and bound across the room. She opens the door and beams up at me.

"Do you like my message?"

She has her hair in babyish pigtails. One is dyed blue and one red. She's wearing too much blush. Sometimes I think she believes she's still five and not eleven. Her tininess doesn't help.

"I don't know what it means," I say. "Explain."

"Enter."

I follow her in and sit on the edge of her bed.

She plops down beside me, then scooches back so she can sit cross-legged. I move back and do the same so we're facing each other.

"I can see your underwear," she tells me.

I push my skirt down between my legs.

"You smell like a boy," she says.

I roll my eyes.

"I hate Ben's cologne."

"Well, you'll never have to smell it again. We broke up."

Instead of clapping, she sighs thoughtfully.

"Well, it was bound to happen," she says matter-of-factly.

"Why do you say that?" I ask.

She props her elbow on her knee and rests her chin in the cup of her hand. A classic Beth pose. She studies me.

"You really are very pretty," she says. "Mom and Dad don't know where the heck you came from."

"Maybe I'm adopted."

"No. You have Dad's eyes and Mom's mouth and nose. They just look better on you."

"Thanks. And don't say that in front of them."

She wrinkles her own nose. "I don't have to. They know it already."

She squinches up the rest of her face. "I used to hate you for it."

This surprises me. "Really?"

She half shrugs. "Who wouldn't? Look at me."

I look. She is not much to look at, if I'm going to be completely honest. She has my parents' features, too, but not the right ones. My dad's square jaw would look OK if Beth was a boy. And my mom's small mouth would look pretty and doll-like except not so much matched with that jaw. Poor Beth.

"Are you going to explain the gold?" I ask to change the subject.

She nods. "It's from a book I read. *The Outsiders.*"

I laugh. "That makes sense," I say sarcastically. "I never was one to fit in."

"No, see. There's this part in the book about staying who you are, no matter what. That's what Ponyboy, the main character, and his best friend Johnny tell each other. 'Stay gold.' It's from a Robert Frost poem."

"Well, aren't you literary."

She smiles.

"Anyway. You know who you are, Grace. You're Grace! You don't change for anyone. I think that's why you're so popular. You know who you want to be. You don't try to be someone you're not. You're gold."

"I may be the popular girl," I say. "But I don't think people like me very much." Is that true? Has that been my fear all along?

Beth tilts her head and squints her eyes at me. "That's dumb. You know they do. You're just feeling insecure right now because of Ben."

"What do you know?" I say. I feel like crying but not in front of her.

"Trust me. I know what it's like when people *really* don't like you. I'm a freak. Only Mom and Dad appreciate my finer qualities. Everyone else just thinks I'm annoying."

"I don't," I say.

"Liar."

"Well, I don't anymore. Now that you think I'm gold." I smile to let her know I'm mostly joking.

"We've never had very strong sister powers," she says. "But I think that could change."

"Why now?"

"Why *not* now?" She motions for me to turn around so my back is facing her.

She gently reaches for my braids and pulls the ties off them. She slowly runs her fingers through my hair to unplait it. I used to do this to her when she was little. I loved to braid her hair and practice different kinds of updos. I'd make her look like a child beauty-pageant contestant. My parents hated it, which, I admit, was my motivation to do it in the first place. I don't know why I have to push their buttons. I guess because they're always pushing mine.

"You have the prettiest hair," she tells me. "If you look closely, it's not just all blond. There are flecks of orange and red and gold. Especially gold."

She tilts my head back and begins to brush it. I can't remember the last time someone brushed my hair for me. My mom or dad must have when I was little, but I don't have any memory of it. They wouldn't have spent this much time if they did. They'd probably do just enough to get the tangles out.

"Remember when you used to dress me up?" Beth asks.

I nod.

"I miss that, I guess," she tells me. "Even though you always tugged on my hair too hard."

"I'm sorry," I tell her. "It's the only way to get a flawless braid."

"Why did you care so much if there was a flaw? It was my hair, not yours."

I smile even though she can't see me. "I know this is going to come as a shock to you, but I'm kind of a perfectionist."

She yanks my hair playfully.

"I guess there's nothing too wrong with wanting to be perfect," she says.

"Little Miss Perfect," I say quietly.

"What?"

"Oh, nothing," I say.

"When I finish, you do me, OK?"

"Sure," I say. "And, Beth?"

"Yeah?"

"I think you're pretty gold, too."

She begins braiding my hair back into place, but I can tell by the halfhearted tugs she's not doing a very good job. The strands will be loose and fall out. Normally, this would make me twitch. I'd pull her hands away and do it myself. But tonight her hands feel like they are doing more than braiding my hair imperfectly. Tonight they feel like she is putting me back together.

A little less perfect than I was before.

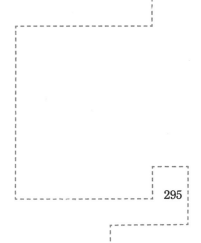

TEN:
READ BETWEEN THE LINES
(Ms. Lindsay: 9:10 p.m.)

I.

IT HAS BEEN A LONG DAY.

Ms. Lindsay undresses in her tiny apartment and slips on her extra-fluffy pink terry-cloth bathrobe. It smells like Downy fabric softener with lavender infusion. She bought it on sale at Target. She read somewhere that the scent of lavender is supposed to relieve stress. She lifts the sleeve to her nose and takes a deep breath, then waits.

Nothing happens.

She's not surprised. It never does.

ı | | ı

The day started like any other. After her shower, Ms. Lindsay dressed in her usual pencil-cut skirt (a gray pinstripe), a silk blouse (violet), and her new black shoes (from the clearance shelf at the Bloomingdale's outlet store). She ate her usual breakfast of a scrambled egg, a slice of toast with apricot jam, and a cup of tea with milk. She flossed and brushed her teeth, inspecting her gums carefully for any overlooked bits. She locked the door and double-checked the handle to make sure all was secure. Then she got in her car and drove to work.

The nausea she always felt as she neared the school welcomed her on Fourth Street and grew in strength when she reached the school parking lot. She cut the engine and sat, breathing slowly and deliberately until her stomach calmed.

"Today will be better," she whispered to herself as she did every morning. "Today will be better," she lied.

It hadn't been better.

The entire day was a struggle all the way up to her very late lunch period, which she spent alone in the quiet teachers' lounge reading a book so she didn't have to talk to anyone.

It didn't help. She did not want to go back into her classroom even after a break from it. She stood outside the door clutching the handle, talking herself into entering.

She breathed in slowly and deeply, like always.

Just one more class to go, Lynnie

You can do this.

She squeezed the handle more tightly. Her heart was racing. Sixth period: the worst class by far. The worst. She had thought the creative writing class would attract the brightest students, but instead it was mostly filled with the ones trying to meet their writing requirement. The ones who assumed creative writing would be the easiest way to do that.

She closed her eyes. No amount of positive self-talk seemed to help. She must go back in. She must. But opening the door was always so hard.

She knew she should be grateful to have a job at all. It took her two years of subbing before she finally landed this one. She couldn't risk losing it. She turned the handle slowly, pushed the door forward as if it was a giant boulder blocking the opening to a dark cave. She felt, for a moment, like Polyphemus returning to a cave of sheep. It wasn't the first time she felt like a monster.

The smell always hit first. The staleness of the room. Perfume, stinky shoes, gum breath. She always choked on it just a little. She always almost cried. In fact, today she *did* cry. Just a few tears. She quickly wiped them away and hurried to her desk, where, thankfully, she had a lavender-scented candle she could inhale the smell of—though, like the fabric softener, it never really seemed to help. It only masked the other nasty smells about to engulf the room, and only barely.

She had ten minutes before class started. Ten minutes to get herself together.

She skimmed through the graded papers on her desk with her green pen, making final notes and grammatical corrections. She always uses a green pen instead of red. She hates red. It's as if the teacher is trying to draw blood on the page. Ms. Lindsay believes green represents growth and possibility.

Not all of the students are terrible writers. Some even have promise. It's their behavior that drives Ms. Lindsay crazy. Their disrespect. Their insistence that she is trying to replace their old teacher, even though they couldn't be more wrong.

When she interviewed with the principal and he told her about the situation, it's true that she began to have second thoughts. The teacher who preceded her had not only died, as she'd first been told, but had committed suicide. This added a whole new layer to the horror of it all, as she'd heard he was fairly young. The principal used the words *tragic* and *mystery* quite a lot to describe what had happened. He had been in his thirties, much older than young Ms. Lindsay, but still too young to die. A well-loved teacher. No one could understand what happened. No one could understand why. Such a tragedy. Such a mystery.

Having worked here now for almost three months, Ms. Lindsay was starting to understand what might have put him over the edge, and it scared her. She'd already had a taste of hopelessness that comes with not being able to make a difference. The despair, knowing some of your students just won't go far, if anywhere.

She'd started that summer. This gave her plenty of time to set up her classroom and develop her own curriculum, though Mr. Weidenheff's was clearly preapproved and she was told she was welcome to use his planners as a base. When she first walked into the classroom, she felt an overwhelming sense of unease. She was sure she could feel Mr. Weidenheff's spirit there, watching her disapprovingly. Someone had been in the room to remove his personal things from the desk, but so much remained. Too much. The corny posters on the wall trying to convey how cool it is to BE A READER. The neatly arranged bookcase in the back of the room stuffed with books that, what? Weren't in the school library? Were Mr. Weidenheff's favorites? She thought morbidly that a dead man had touched them all. His now-dead hands had arranged the desks. Had—she shuddered—written the words that remained on the whiteboard. Someone had forgotten to erase them. Or, perhaps, been unable to bring themselves to do it.

"You can make a stack of all the things you'd like to get rid of," the principal told her. "And we'll take care of them." He said this sadly, and she knew he hoped she wouldn't get rid of a thing.

She'd spent the next week moving everything to the center of the room and starting fresh. First the bookcases. She was fond of many of the books she found there and took care to rearrange them in alphabetical order by author, not title, as he had done. She wondered for days whether or not to cross out the letters written in black marker across the head of each book, WEIDENHEFF. When she'd suggested the library take them, it turned out they were all duplicates. "No room," the librarian had said sadly. But Ms. Lindsay got the sense that it had more to do with the morbid name at the top of each book than space.

She wished she had her own books to add to the collection. But the only ones she had were from her adolescence, and they were too precious to share. She couldn't possibly risk having a student take one home and not return it. She couldn't. Did that make her worse than Mr. Weidenheff? She hoped not. Someday, when she could

302

afford to buy duplicates, she would. She made a promise to herself at that very moment.

She moved the desk to a different corner and changed where the phone and computer were placed. She scrubbed each drawer and top, even though they were empty and mostly clean. She put the student desks in a new configuration. She took a deep breath and erased the board. She took down all the tacky posters. She swept and mopped the floor herself. And when she was done, she stood in the doorway and imagined how the students would see the room. Would it feel different enough? Had she removed all the traces of Mr. Weidenheff? She glanced at the bookcase again and saw his name all along the tops of the books. Over and over again. A reminder. What could she do about that, though? She couldn't possibly throw the books away or blacken out his name. No. But . . . what? She had no idea who else to ask. So she left them. Books were the one thing she knew the value of.

She's calculated that it would be three more years after this one before the students who knew Mr. Weidenheff would graduate, and then it wouldn't be so hard to be the "tragically dead teacher's replacement." Sure, new students would know *of* him, through older siblings or school folklore. But none of them would have had him for a teacher. None of them would be able to make the comparisons that all the current students made. None of them would have the same loyalty.

Each month, she slowly replaced a few more Weidenheff books on the bookcase with ones she bought herself. She found most of them used online for fairly cheap, and sometimes she bought three or four at a time to save on postage. It would take time, but someday all the books would say LINDSAY in green marker instead of WEIDENHEFF in black. Already, if you looked across the room at the shelves, you could see pretty green letters mixed between the lines of black, and this made her happy. Hopeful.

She tried to cling to that just before sixth period, as she waited for her class to begin filtering in, but her thoughts drifted to the weekend.

II.

It started with a date on Friday night that she would rather not remember, and dinner at a bar on Saturday night with the one teacher she's managed to befriend,

Betsy Yung. It was Betsy's idea to go have some fun. Betsy has been teaching computer classes at Irving for over six years. She took Ms. Lindsay under her wing when she'd been hired to take over poor Mr. Weidenheff's classroom. Both are single and, she knows, the subjects of gossip and speculation about whether or not they're a "couple."

The rumor also includes a love-triangle conspiracy with Ms. Sawyer, the gym teacher. But Betsy assured Ms. Lindsay that Ms. Sawyer is straighter than a flagpole and it just figures the idiots in this school would assume the female gym teacher must be a "lesbo." Betsy's word, not Ms. Lindsay's.

There's nothing to the gossip.

Ms. Lindsay finds Betsy dull and crass and not anything like the type of woman she would fall for, if she were to fall for a woman. Which she isn't likely to do, no matter how repeatedly dull and disappointing her dates with men have been so far.

No. Ms. Lindsay has come to accept that she will most likely always be single, short of some miracle. Let the gossipers gossip.

She and Betsy often sit at lunch in the teachers' room, sighing frequently and heavily at the thought of going back to the Little Devils, as Betsy calls them. Betsy hates them, clearly. With Ms. Lindsay, It isn't so much hate as . . . well, what is it, actually? Resentment? Fear? She can't decide.

Betsy informed her that Mr. Weidenheff wasn't even all that popular. Especially with the loser-track kids (Betsy's horrible term for the students no one expects to go to college). But his death has made him a hero somehow. This was all very dangerous territory. A suicide was never to be given too much focus at a school, for fear others would see it as a way of getting attention. Did the administrators really think anyone was dumb enough not to realize that you'd never know about the attention if you were dead? Apparently not. In any case, no one is allowed to discuss "the incident." If a student brings it up, teachers are not to talk about it in class but must tell the student to go to the school counselor to discuss it in private. As if any student would do that. They want to talk about it *together*. But rules are rules. Maybe that's why they hate her. Because Ms. Lindsay, if nothing else, is a rule follower.

So it's hard. Very hard. To stand in front of a group of teenagers who don't respect her because she refuses to buck the system by talking about the elephant in the room. Or, more precisely, the ghost.

And it's not just that. She's heard the boys whisper about what she'd look like without her pencil skirt and about her just low-enough blouse to give them a sense that there's something worth seeing underneath. They admire her, but through resentful eyes. This doesn't help her status with the girls, who certainly know Ms. Lindsay's body is "hotter" than theirs if only because it's unattainable, which just makes the boys more interested. Why are adolescent boys so turned on by lesbians? It is a mystery Ms. Lindsay doesn't care about enough to solve.

Somehow, in the students' eyes, it seems the only thing Ms. Lindsay has to offer besides inappropriate fantasies and assumptions is a passing grade to help them on to their next miserable year. You don't have to show much respect to earn that. Which is why she doesn't get any. Instead, she finds female condoms left in her desk drawer. The occasional DYKE left on the whiteboard when she arrives in the morning. And the nearly impossible task of having a meaningful class discussion about literature or writing. It is torture.

No one likes to be hated.

It isn't what Ms. Lindsay envisioned when she decided to be a teacher. She thought the experience would be like her favorite old movie, *To Sir, with Love.* The students would adore her and confide in her. *To Miss, with Love.* She would inspire them to be more than the nobodies the rest of the world felt sure they'd become.

But no. That's not how it turned out at all.

She had talked about all of these things over dinner at the bar with Betsy on Saturday night, which surprised her. Normally Betsy did the talking. But the glass of sauvignon blanc had made Ms. Lindsay chatty. And for whatever reason, Betsy, up to that point, sat quietly and listened.

"Do you think things will ever change?" Ms. Lindsay asked her friend.

Betsy shook her head. "They never change. Every year it's more of the same. Ungrateful little fuckers."

She hissed the last too loudly, and a couple sitting nearby gave them dirty looks. Betsy glared at them, then laughed. A small speck of lettuce spewed from her mouth and landed on Ms. Lindsay's unused fork.

Ms. Lindsay turned the fork over.

She thought of the conference she'd been forced to attend two weekends before in order to earn professional development points. The speech had been about crowd control and getting a handle on your classroom. The talk seemed meant for elementary-school teachers, and Ms. Lindsay's mind had wandered through most of it, knowing the techniques would just get more laughs from her class. "This is the 'quiet down' cymbol," the woman said, looking seriously at the audience. She held up her hand and made what Ms. Lindsay was sure was the Girl Scout pledge sign. "When I do this, the students know it means to be quiet and listen."

Ms. Lindsay had closed her eyes and pressed her temples with the same three fingers. Her head had started to throb.

"If only they'd listen to me," Ms. Lindsay confided to Betsy. "But it's all I can do to keep them quiet, much less absorb anything I have to say."

"Tell them to shut the fuck up," Betsy said, sending another speck of green jetting across their tall bar table. Why were tables at bars always so uncomfortable? They were sitting on tall stools, and Ms. Lindsay felt that one more glass of wine and she'd be at a very high risk of toppling to the floor.

"That's what we should all do," Betsy continued. "You need to tell them who's boss, Lynnette."

Ms. Lindsay cringed. She hated the sound of her full name. No one called her that. They called her Lynne. Lynne Lindsay. It was a ridiculous name, but Lynnette was even worse. Unfortunately, Betsy thought her name was amusing and old-fashioned and couldn't seem to stop saying it. Now it was her little joke, which Ms. Lindsay never thought was funny.

"I swear one day I will," Betsy said. "I don't care if I get fired."

"Yes, you do," Ms. Lindsay said, bored of hearing it all again. "We all do. That's why nothing changes."

"You're such a downer," Betsy said. She pushed the rest of her salad to the middle of her plate with her fork and scooped up the last heaving mouthful.

Ms. Lindsay sipped her expensive glass of wine. It was a label the waiter had suggested. Kim Crawford. He had winked at her when she took her first sip. Ms. Lindsay wondered blankly who Kim Crawford was. She imagined Ms. Crawford's life was far more interesting than her own.

As soon as he left the table, Betsy said their waiter was gay. Why, Ms. Lindsay wondered, were so many people obsessed with people's sexuality?

"By the way," Betsy said, leaning closer, "you haven't told me how your date with the janitor was last night." She made a disapproving face.

When Ms. Lindsay had told her that he'd asked her out, Betsy had roared with laughter. This response alone made Ms. Lindsay tell him yes.

That was a mistake.

Ms. Lindsay shrugged. "I don't really want to talk about it," she said. She really did not want to relive that night.

"Oh, come on," Betsy had pressed. "Did you hook up?"

"No! God, no."

"Where did you eat?"

"A little Italian place in the city."

"Well, *that* sounds romantic."

Ms. Lindsay had thought so, too. When he told her where to meet, she'd immediately looked up the restaurant's website and scoured the menu.

They'd sat at a tiny table with a red-and-white-checked tablecloth. Ms. Lindsay thought it mostly *was* romantic, at least at first. She kept thinking about the scene from a Disney movie she'd loved as a child. What was it? There were dogs, she remembered. And they were eating pasta at a little table, just like this. It had a checkered tablecloth too. But they were eating from the same bowl. Spaghetti. And at one point they were eating from different ends of the same piece, and as they kept slurping the string, their snouts got closer and closer to each other and then they kissed. Or touched noses. Dogs don't really kiss. *Lady and the Tramp*. That's what it was called.

Thinking of the dogs, Ms. Lindsay had looked up at Jared French's nose and wondered what it would be like to kiss him. His nose wasn't too bad. Not too big. It probably wouldn't get in the way. She wasn't sure about the beard though. She wasn't sure how she felt about it, even though it was thin and seemed carefully trimmed. It was almost *too* trimmed. And it was . . . well, it was weird. He had what was sort of a goatee, but he also had a little square patch of hair under his bottom lip. It bothered her.

She recalled the term *soul patch* and wondered if that's what it was. She studied him, wondering about his soul. But she was having trouble getting past the beard. She'd never kissed someone with a beard. Actually, she hadn't had much practice in the kissing department at all lately.

Ms. Lindsay was shy. She was also picky. She hadn't had many dating opportunities since she started teaching full-time, and she'd been beginning to feel lonely. Even so, her first reaction to Jared's invitation was *no*. She'd said she would get back to him so she could think about it. Then she'd gone to get Betsy's advice and was so bothered by her reaction, she'd decided to say yes.

"He doesn't drink," Ms. Lindsay confided in Betsy, who was sipping her third Cadillac margarita. This concoction, Betsy explained, was a margarita with an extra shot of Grand Marnier. Like two drinks in one. Ms. Lindsay had done the math and was surprised Betsy was still able to balance on the bar stool.

Betsy choked on her Cadillac. "Why not?"

"He's a recovering alcoholic."

"You don't say."

"We spent most of the night talking about it," Ms. Lindsay explained. "He's had a pretty tough life. I asked him what made him get sober, and do you know what he said?"

Betsy waited.

"He hit a deer with his car. He was driving drunk and hit it. And then he left the scene without seeing if it was dead or alive."

"*That's* what sobered him up?" Betsy asked incredulously. "Either that guy is the most sensitive bastard on earth or he's lying."

Ms. Lindsay nodded. As she recalled the conversation, she remembered thinking something similar. In fact, as she listened to him go on and on as if she were his AA sponsor, she almost had the sense that Jared hadn't been talking about hitting a deer at all. He talked about it as if he'd done something far worse and uncommon. "I've never told anyone this before," he said quietly. "I don't know why I'm telling you. I probably shouldn't." It had made her feel uncomfortable. Scared, even.

"She left behind a child," he told her. Ms. Lindsay asked if he meant a fawn, and he looked confused. "Yes. A fawn. You . . . you remind me of her." Ms. Lindsay looked confused again. She reminded him of a fawn? Well, she did have big eyes. She smiled awkwardly at the strange compliment. But Jared only seemed to be getting more agitated. At this point Ms. Lindsay wondered if Jared French was on medication. He was so upset. So confused. "Why am I telling you this?" he kept asking. He had stopped being able to look at her. And that was when Ms. Lindsay suggested they call it a night.

"Did you pay or go dutch?" Betsy asked, not nearly as disturbed by the story as Ms. Lindsay had been.

"Dutch."

"Figures."

"Well, I probably make more than him, so it's only fair. Plus, I had a glass of wine."

"How insensitive!" Betsy had covered her mouth in mock disapproval.

"I ordered it before I knew he didn't drink!" Ms. Lindsay protested. "I ended up having one sip. It was so awkward. We paid and went our separate ways."

"What will you do on Monday?"

"Try to avoid him."

Betsy shook her head. "I told you not to go."

Ms. Lindsay did not argue. She also didn't mention the awkward good-bye she'd had with him when they went outside. They'd stood under the streetlight, both probably wondering how to end it. In the light, she'd noticed a crumb of Italian bread in his beard patch. She hoped it would fall out before he discovered it himself, when he went to brush his teeth and get ready for bed that evening. She wondered what his reaction would be at the discovery. Would he laugh? Blush? Be horrified? She wasn't sure.

She said good night and thank you. And he apologized for going on and on about his own problems and not asking her much about herself, though he still couldn't seem to look at her.

"Oh, me, I'm boring," she'd said.

She reached out to shake his hand, which felt like a stupid thing to do, but she didn't want to kiss him, that was certain. But instead of taking her hand, he moved out of the way and said good night, rushing down the sidewalk.

It was such a strange moment, Ms. Lindsay didn't

even know how to retell it. And besides, she didn't want to share the "boring" comment with Betsy, who would surely agree.

"What exciting lives we lead," Betsy said, signaling for the check.

The waiter, who was decidedly not gay, divided their bill. Ms. Lindsay did not tell Betsy he'd written his phone number on her customer copy. And while she wondered, just briefly, if he'd done the same on Betsy's bill, she quickly dismissed the thought. She was sure Betsy would have pointed it out.

"See you on Monday with the beasts," Betsy had said when they parted ways outside.

"Don't remind me," Ms. Lindsay replied.

"Little fuckers," she heard Betsy mutter as she walked away.

On the way home, Ms. Lindsay stopped at the liquor outlet and bought a bottle of pinot noir from the sale display. She put on her pajamas, opened her laptop, and watched a movie in bed.

It was not the best girls' night out.

It never was.

III.

And then on Monday there she was, barely making it through the day, and certainly not the start of sixth period. Ms. Lindsay had sighed and looked at the clock. She had two more minutes before the students would come pushing through the door. She wasn't sure why she'd been thinking about her dinner with Betsy Yung. It wasn't particularly eye-opening and certainly wasn't inspiring. But maybe that was just it. When she got home that night, she had promised herself she would not turn into Betsy. She would not. She would not be bitter. She had also decided to be on the lookout for Jared French today and try to be friendly. But so far, he was nowhere to be seen. Maybe he was the one avoiding her. Either way. She was going to be kind. Positive.

That was her plan. This morning, she had tried to feel hopeful. She got up early so she could take an extra-long shower. She carefully lathered her hair with her awapuhi shampoo that smelled like Hawaii, which was the only tropical place she'd ever visited. She had been eleven and still young enough for her wealthy grandmother to think she was cute and a nice thing to take along with her on vacations to impress her other elderly friends. Tiny

Lynnette (she allowed her grandmother to call her this because she loved her) had spent most of the week by herself, wandering around the hotel pool while her grandmother played cards with two old men she'd met. "This is Lynn-ette," her grandmother told them.

"Ligh-net?" one man had asked in a horrible southern drawl.

"Goodness, no. *Lynn*-ette. *LYNN!* Just for that horrible pronunciation, you will buy me a drink."

Lynn-ette never forgot the smell in the air as she walked past the plants and shrubs lining the pathways at the hotel. That sweet, pungent smell of flowers and nectar. And the beautiful poolside bartender who smiled at her in a sexy way and made her feel attractive for the first time in her life. Even if she had only been eleven. She wondered how old he was. Maybe in his early twenties? It wasn't so wrong of him, was it? It was the best vacation of her life. As soon as she was hired for this full-time job, she'd started saving to return, though her grandmother had died years ago. She didn't mind planning a trip alone. Maybe that bartender would still be there. She could dream. What else was there?

She looked at the clock again. Twenty seconds. She thought of the bartender's hungry smile, but to her dismay his face quickly morphed into Jared's, with the broad crumb in his beard. She wasn't going to allow herself to think about their date, and here she was, already remembering again. *Jared.* She shuddered. What was she thinking?

She took another calming breath, but it didn't help. She felt the fear building so strongly, her heart began to race. It pounded and hurt with each beat.

It was time.

The students filed in, pushing each other from one seat to another. Joking. Laughing. Checking out what she was wearing without even trying not to be obvious. Ms. Lindsay cowered behind her desk, ashamed.

As usual, she lost her positive outlook three minutes into class.

The chaos only built.

Tanner G. leaned forward and flicked Tanner F.'s ear with his finger, turning it purple-red. Tanner F. tried not to cry. Ms. Lindsay cleared her throat and was ignored. She took more slow deep breaths and thought of Betsy's words. For the first time she looked out at her students and thought the vile phrase. *Little fuckers.*

She didn't want to feel that way about them. She wanted to love them. But as Alicia Crowley pushed her chest out at Max Findlay, who reached forward and pretended he was going to pinch her nipples, Ms. Lindsay decided enough was enough.

"Quiet!" she yelled. Her heart was really racing now, and she wondered what it would take to have a heart attack. She could feel it out-beating the second hand on the big wall clock by four to one. Her students looked at her and waited. She breathed and felt her chest rise up and down, then caught Cal Hogan staring at her breasts, which, she realized, could easily be thought of as "heaving."

"We're going to try something different today," she said, trying to sound stern. Serious. Her eyes moved from face to face. She thought she saw Sapphie Lewis roll her eyes, but it was hard to get a good look at her face—hidden, as always, under the hood of her sweatshirt. Keith Sears studied her thoughtfully, as if he sincerely cared what this something different would be. At least one of them cared, she thought.

Then, interrupting her big moment, Nate Granger entered late. He waved his late pass and held up his hand as if he had a question, but on further inspection she realized he was holding it up because he had a splint on his finger. His middle finger.

Cal, sitting nearby, snickered.

"It's Finger Boy!" someone whispered loudly as Nate took his seat.

He did look like he was giving them all the finger. She felt her mouth twist into a smirk. Good for him. She'd seen him bullied all fall. Now he had some respect. So long as he didn't aim that finger at her.

She waited for him to sit and get settled, then looked at them all as they waited for whatever this something was she wanted to try. She felt a mixture of disgust and ownership, knowing it was up to her to change their ways. Up to her to make them respect her. Not out of fear, but because she'd earned it. She wanted, she realized, for them to like her.

But Ms. Lindsay was also realistic. She knew, at that moment, as one kid picked his nose without shame and another fiddled with her phone right out in the open even though it was against school rules and Allen Quimby mouthed the words *I want you* to the girl across the aisle—that they never would.

They just didn't care.

"You know I have a soft voice," Ms. Lindsay went on, trying to use a loud voice, "so from now on when I want your attention I'm going to do this." Ms. Lindsay raised her hand in the Girl Scout pledge, just like the woman from her discipline workshop. As she did, she remembered the Girl Scout promise she made as a child.

On my honor, I will try to serve God and my country, to help people at all times, and to live by the Girl Scout Law.

If only she could remember the Girl Scout Law. Was the Girl Scout Law simply to try to serve God and her country, and to help people at all times? She wasn't sure. She had failed as a Girl Scout, clearly. She'd only lasted two years. That was how long her mother had put up with taking her to all the meetings and sewing all the patches on her uniform sash and ironing her uniform and making sure she had the proper color knee socks. Until, in her mother's words, it was too much, and Lynnette was "too old for that stuff anyway."

The class continued to watch her intently, almost eagerly, as if they thought the moment had come at last when perhaps they had finally succeeded in driving her over the edge. Had they learned nothing from Mr. Weidenheff? Why was she so different? Instead of sympathy, grief, and sadness, there was satisfaction in their eyes. Glee. They were quiet. Waiting.

The moment was brief, but time had stopped.

She searched again for someone to connect with. Her eyes settled on Nate Granger. *Finger Boy.* He smiled at her, and she summoned one more ounce of courage.

She stared at her three fingers raised in the air and was surprised to have another quick childhood memory, this time of her mother, years ago, getting so upset with her father, she thought her mother's eyes would pop out of their sockets. But even in her fit of rage, her mother could not bring herself to curse. "Read between the lines, Harold!" she'd hissed, holding up three fingers and glaring at him. Her father's mouth dropped open first in shock, and then hilarity, as he burst out laughing at her ridiculousness. "Just say the words, you old fool!" he'd shouted back. "My God, you're a prude."

Her mother burst into tears. Her father made it clear he could care less. He pushed back his chair and stomped out of the room, leaving her mother sitting at the end of the table with her shoulders shaking, tears slipping down her cheeks. And quiet little Lynnette in the middle, with no idea what to do.

It wasn't until the next day when she asked her best friend Rose what it could have meant that she learned her mother was giving her father the finger. And what giving someone the finger meant.

Ms. Lindsay looked at her three slender fingers facing the class. She looked at her students, staring back at her with curiosity and—could it be?—amazement. Slowly, she turned her hand from the pledge position to the sign her mother had used all those years ago.

Read between the lines, class, she whispered in her head. *Ef you.*

Yes, she really thought *ef* and not the F-word. Her mother had a big impression on her after all. She didn't care that her father would laugh at her, too, if he could see her. To Ms. Lindsay, her mother had shown the greatest restraint. That was class. She stuck to her morals in the face of great adversity. And so, now, would Ms. Lindsay. She even felt some of her old Girl Scout pride. Was there a badge for that?

She held her three fingers firmly in the air and marveled at the silence and the curious looks on the faces of those who simply didn't understand what they'd missed out on, if only they could have given her half a chance. She could have been a great teacher. *To Miss, with Love.* But no. They never even gave her a chance to try.

The little fuckers.

No.

No, she wouldn't sink to Betsy's low.

For now, she heard and repeated her mother's words in her head instead.

Read between the lines, class.

"It means the F-word," Rose had told her in a whisper.

"What does *that* mean?" innocent Lynnette had whispered back.

"It means I hate you," Rose told her. And then, seeing the look of horror on poor Lynnette's face at the thought of her mother telling her father she hated him, Rose changed her mind. "No, I mean, it means I'm really, really mad at you."

Sweet Lynnette had nodded. "Oh," she said, and accepted the misinformation for two more years, until she learned the true meaning of the rude gesture.

Read between the lines, class, she thought again, knowing full well that she was more than really, really mad at them.

They looked at her, confused.

It felt good.

Did they know what she was doing? She was sure not. They simply continued to peer at her curiously and watch.

Read between the lines.

She hesitated another moment, for effect, and then slowly lowered her hand.

"Well," she said happily. "Good. That seems to work."

She turned and walked to her desk, trying not to smile. Trying not to laugh.

"Everyone get out your writing journals, please," Ms. Lindsay instructed before she sat down.

To her amazement, they did.

IV.

Now, as she sniffs the lavender-scented sleeve of her bathrobe hopelessly, Ms. Lindsay feels guilty for giving her crowded class of bored teenagers the finger. She even starts to cry. For not being able to make a difference. For not even getting close to achieving the respect she's worked so hard for, has hoped for, all her life. She cries, and then begins to run a hot bath, emptying the entire bottle of awapuhi shampoo into the water to surround herself with the smell—forget the useless lavender—and the Hawaiian memories of one good time. Of a time full of hope and wonder and being loved, if only superficially and for selfish purposes, by her grandmother.

She settles into the tub and leans back as the warm, comforting water slowly covers her body like a blanket. The sound of the water hides the chirp of her phone ringing in the next room. It is the school guidance counselor letting her know about the day's happenings, so that she might be prepared to help the students cope tomorrow. She explains that Stephen Holland's father had a heart attack and is in stable condition at Mount Ivy Hospital; that Jared French (the janitor, she notes, as if Ms. Lindsay might not know who he is) appears to have had some sort of mental break and was found on the side of the highway but was also taken to Mount Ivy Hospital for observation; and that Keith Sears had been hit by a car—*hit-and-run, the poor kid*—and wouldn't be in school the next two days because he had a mild concussion. There is a pause and the sound of a breath being exhaled. Of disappointment perhaps, that Ms. Lindsay isn't available to gossip about all of this with her. Maybe they could have bonded over it and become friends. "What a wacky day," she says, to end the one-sided conversation. "We'll have a faculty meeting first thing in the morning to discuss how to handle things. Have a good night!" But Ms. Lindsay won't get the message until the next morning, when the night will already be over.

As the water rises to her neck, Ms. Lindsay closes her eyes, surrounded by the smell of her Hawaiian vacation memories. She sees that bartender in her mind's eye, and this time he does not morph into Jared French and his ridiculous beard. No. He remains her beautiful Hawaiian boy, with his white-toothed smile, the dark dimples in the middle of his cheeks. His green, mischievous eyes.

I remember you, she tells him, speaking into the sudsy water.

I remember.

I remember you.

I remember how you made me feel.

And in that moment, even though it is brief, she remembers just enough to feel that way again.

When she rises out of the water, the dream will float away with the fading scent of awapuhi, replaced with the reality that she will have to go back to school tomorrow. Back to the stares and the gossip and the not listening. But somehow, Ms. Lindsay remains hopeful, despite what she knows. She will drive to school and sit in the parking lot and make the same promise she always makes, even if she doesn't necessarily believe it.

Today will be better.

She will stand in front of the class and hold up her three fingers to quiet them down, and for a moment she will think, *Read between the lines, class.*

But then, as she looks at their unsuspecting, uninterested faces, she will start to think about what that really means. That just like there is more to her than what they see, there is more inside each one of them.

What's your story? she will wonder as she scans the room from face to face.

And this time, when she pleads with them to read between the lines, she will try to do the same.

ACKNOWLEDGMENTS

I am grateful to my writing partners, Cindy Faughnan and Debbi Michiko Florence, for their love and support and valuable feedback. To Robin Wasserman, who forced me to send her chapters to prove I really was still working on this project I was writing "just for fun." To my agent, Barry Goldblatt, who didn't laugh when I told him my dream, but instead said, "Write it!" To my husband, Peter Carini, and my son, Eli Carini, who listened to my ideas and brainstormed with me through countless dinners. I love and appreciate you both so much. And finally, to my wonderful editor, Joan Powers, who embraced this project and always inspires me to tell it true, no matter what. Thank you for giving me the courage to write the stories my heart longs to tell.